Longi

Stuntman-heartthrob Tate Sinclair is every woman's dream guy: he's gorgeous, adventurous, and successful as a movie stuntman and adventure seeker. Gigi Mason isn't immune to his good looks but she is immune to the wanderlust in his veins. She's been burned before by a walk-away-Joe kind of guy who chose the call of the wild over a life with her. And she's determined it won't ever happen again.

After a close call on a movie set plagued with trouble, Tate returns to Sunset Bay for his brother Brad's wedding. Love is in the air all around him and he's feeling torn by this new tug toward wanting a love of his own. When he finds Gigi in an embarrassing situation and rescues her, his interest is stirred...but she's not interested in him and makes it more than clear.

Tate was born loving a challenge and Gigi is about to find out that he's not that easy to ignore...the more she tells him she's not interested, the more he's determined to change her mind.

But is it the love of a challenge or actually love?

LONGING FOR YOU

Sunset Bay Romance, Book Five

DEBRA CLOPTON

Longing for You

Copyright © 2019 Debra Clopton Parks

CHAPTER ONE

Hiding behind a giant potted plant at his brother's wedding reception was not Tate Sinclair's idea of fun. Being stuck with torn tendons in his ankle from his latest movie stunt gone wrong and now wearing a rehab boot with his tux was also not the way he'd hoped to celebrate his brother's happy day. Answering endless questions about the boot had grown old after the first thirty minutes of his arrival. But the worst of all was the endless questions asking when he was going to find a good girl, stop his gallivanting all over the world, settle down and have a house full of babies to make his mother happy—yep, that was the worst of the not-fun host of questions of the evening. The questions that had finally driven him to the dark corner behind the plant for a little quiet time.

And also, a last-resort preventative measure to keep him from saying something he might regret. Everyone meant well, but that still didn't make it any easier to handle.

Peeking through the palm's leaves, he watched Brad and Lulu, the newlyweds, dancing their hearts out, looking as happy as they should be. Surrounded by family and friends, celebrating full swing. Looking at them, he suddenly felt like he was on the outside looking in...

Disjointed—or a better word, he admitted to himself, would be dissatisfied.

Watching Brad and Lulu exchange vows earlier and seeing the love shining between them had heaped another strong dose of longing spilling through him.

Longing...yes, that was what he felt. He was pretty blindsided by the feeling, and yet as he'd watched his other brothers and their new wives and his sister Erin and her fiancé dancing, Tate had slowly started to feel that maybe he was ready to look for someone with whom to share his life.

It had also been frustrating when people had automatically assumed he would just find a wife and settle down too. Life didn't happen like clockwork. You couldn't just wish for love and get it instantly.

A door slammed behind him, not loud enough for the partygoers to hear over the music but loud enough for him to hear from his position. As he spun to see what was going on there was a yelp. He was startled to see one of the bridesmaids standing at the end of the hall with her back to him.

"You've got to be kidding me," the brunette declared in horror as she stared at the restroom door where the ripped off back section of her dress now hung limply and raggedly from the door and the doorframe.

Tate's eyes widened as he got a clear view of long legs and bright-red panties visible from the missing back section of her dress—*"Whoa, how had that happened*—" he said, completely shocked.

At his words she spun quickly and her gaze collided with his. Just as he thought, it was Gigi Mason.

"Tate," she gasped and slapped her hands to her skirt, trying to hide her exposed backside, despite the fact that he could no longer see it.

She was an old classmate from high school who now worked at the Bake My Day bakery owned by his sister-in-law, Rosie. They had spoken briefly earlier before the wedding, but that was about it as he was busy with answering questions and he hadn't made it in for the rehearsal dinner, where he would have spent time with the wedding party. He hadn't gotten used to her dark hair, since she'd had it blonde the last few times he'd seen her when he'd been in town.

Trying to hide a grin and lost as he nodded toward the door. "It looks like you might have a bit of a problem." From her expression she wasn't exactly taking the fact that her dress was half gone very well. Or it could have been because she was probably feeling a draft where she didn't want one.

"Yes. A bad one." She frowned, then her lips

twitched. "Stop grinning, this is not good."

He hitched a brow. "If I had a suit jacket, I'd lend it to you, but as you can see, all I have is the shirt I'm wearing. I could give you that." He reached for the top button of his shirt.

She held out a hand. "No, stop. You can't go walking around without a shirt any more than I can walk around with my rump showing. I don't want to mess up Lulu and Brad's reception with us both being exhibitionists."

He laughed. She was cute. He'd seen her working at Rosie's on occasions when he'd been in town, but he'd been preoccupied with family during his short visits and hadn't really noticed her. Now he was noticing her wholeheartedly.

He unbuttoned the top button, teasing her. "It's not like I haven't gone without a shirt before. But wait— you're afraid seeing my bulging muscles will cause you to faint and everyone will see your red undies?"

She laughed softly. "Um, judging by the way that shirt is stretching across your muscles, *some* of the ladies might faint at the sight of them and disturb the wedding completely. And if I go walking around with your shirt, everybody's going to be looking at me, so maybe you should keep it on."

"You know how to deflate a fella's ego. So, any ideas how we can get you to safety without you flashing the wedding attendees?"

She nibbled at her lip. Her gaze went to the dress-eating door then the dancers then back to him. Her eyes focused and widened. "Are you hiding behind that potted palm bush?"

He stood up straighter, embarrassed, but with no way out. "Yeah, guilty as charged."

"Why? No, wait—they're plastering you with," she did air quotes, "When are you getting married questions and giving Maryetta grandbabies?"

"You're good. Do you moonlight as a detective?"

"Hardly. I saw you cornered up by Lila, Mami, Birdie, and Doreen. Those four are always full of questions. And I overheard someone asking your mom when you were going to settle down. So," she grimaced, "the plight of the single at weddings."

"You are a detective."

"Again, not so much. I get the same questions. I've been hiding out in the ladies' room."

He laughed. "No kidding?"

"Yeah. I finally talked myself into coming out and heading home, and then this happens. I was just staying long enough to wish Lulu and Brad forever happiness. Weddings aren't really my thing."

"Mine either, but with all my siblings busy getting married and engaged, I'm having a busy year."

She smiled and he liked the way it lifted the corners of her eyes. "Yes, you are. Oh, I have an idea—come here."

"Okay." He limped from behind the plant toward her, more exasperated than ever about his ankle injury. "At your service. What may I do for you?"

"I need you to stick to me like glue." She suddenly spun so that he was behind her. She grabbed his hands and yanked him close against her. He was startled but he wasn't one to complain as she looked up at him, slightly over her shoulder. "Now we walk. You just stick close like this and we'll walk out of the building and to my car."

"You mean waddle." He grinned down at her. She fit him perfectly, not too much shorter than him, so their legs were similar lengths, making her plan pretty easy to accomplish, if it weren't for the boot on his injured ankle.

"Try not to waddle too much."

She clung to his hands and he was very aware that she was all female. "You don't think people are going to notice that we're plastered together like wallpaper as we walk through the crowd toward the door?"

Worry flashed through her incredible eyes. Blue-green with navy irises. "They might notice, b-but there's plenty of people out there plastered together like this. Well, maybe not back to front like this, but you know what I'm saying. It's a wedding and they're all out there dancing. We'll just move through there, swaying to the music some and maybe nobody will notice us."

"I guess if that's what you want, I can do that. Do you think I should snuggle you up closer?" He couldn't help picking on her, leaning closer, and realized she smelled delicious, like strawberries or peaches.

Something sweet and fruity. She was really cute and he wasn't sure whether she was thinking exactly straight, but then again, at the moment, he wasn't either. He snuggled her closer to him. She turned her head and looked up at him, her eyes wide as they locked with his. She blinked hard. Their lips were so close he could move slightly and kiss her. Ridiculous notion, but chemistry buzzed between them. *Not the time or place.*

He mustered up his self-control. "Either talk or move. You're going to have to lead the way. Or we'll really give people something to talk about, hiding out back here together snuggled up like this." And he wasn't joking, not one little bit. Rumors were going to roll no matter what after they stepped out of the shadows like this. But what the heck—rumors might stop some of the irritating questions.

* * *

Gigi could not believe she had actually grabbed Tate and plastered herself against him like she'd done. Of all people to find standing there, watching her

9

embarrassing moment, it had to be *him*. Stunning, magnificent, totally unattainable him.

Stuntman extraordinaire, adventure-seeking Tate Sinclair. Her heart fluttered just thinking about him… And now he had his arms wrapped around her, snuggled up close, and she'd completely hijacked him to help in her escape plan. But he smelled so good, he very nearly made her dizzy. And she would not feel bad about using him to get out of here without showing her red panties to the entire wedding crowd.

Her heart thundered as they waddle-walked slowly together toward the door. They had to skirt the dancing crowd and weave through the tables before they could make their escape.

"It looks like an obstacle course," she muttered, distracted by the hard body practically wrapped around her.

"It's getting interesting," Tate said, close to her ear.

His breath feathered against her ear and sent shivers through her.

Of all the people to find her in this predicament.

Nobody knew how big of a thing she had for this guy. She had hidden it all through school, knowing she didn't stand a chance, and she had too much going on at home to even let herself dream of any kind of relationship with any boy, much less Tate Sinclair. Even then, his need for adventure was apparent and it took him away from Sunset Bay right after graduation.

From all accounts through the years of his amazing life—globetrotting around, being photographed doing stunts on movie sets or for photoshoots for magazines, or his own adventures that he caught on camera himself or with a crew—the man led an unbelievably interesting life. Wanderlust was a part of him. And that was more than enough reason for Gigi to keep her secret crush on the guy to herself.

She didn't do wanderlust.

She'd just suffered two shocks in a row: half her dress being ripped off and then turning around to find the object of her unrequited love staring at her.

Tate Sinclair staring at *her*, with that sexy half grin that had long ago caused her insides to do all kinds of acrobatics inside her chest. *Long ago* being the key words here, she again reminded herself. This was not high school. He was simply helping her get out of a sticky situation.

"Now what?" he asked, in that silky voice, jerking her back from her thoughts.

"I don't want to interrupt this wedding. I don't want to take anything away from Brad and Lulu's night, so it's time to stick close. I don't want my—" She clammed up.

He chuckled. "You don't want to show off those red undies? I get it."

"I don't want to talk about them either."

"Your face was priceless when you whirled around, realizing I was there."

She glared up at him, their faces far too close for comfort. "Okay, enough. Let's walk. I don't want to reminisce with you about my red underwear. I'm not happy about you seeing them. You shouldn't have been looking down. You should've been looking at my eyes."

"Hey, I didn't know what you were doing. You had your back to me and you were missing a very important section of your dress. I wasn't expecting to get an eyeful of red panties and tanned skin."

"What do you mean, tan skin? How much did you see?"

"I didn't see anything."

"Yes, you did. How else do you know I have a tan?"

"Your *face* is tanned. Your *arms* are tanned. I'm only assuming that your legs are tanned too."

Her eyes narrowed—and her cheeks burned with embarrassment. Gritting her teeth and needing him despite her embarrassment, she tugged him closer, if that was possible. "Whatever. Here we go. Time for you to be glue." She took a step and held on to his hands as tight as she could, forcing him to move with her. Forcing herself to not think about being cuddled up against him.

And that was a losing battle. Because if there was one thing she knew as of the instant she'd spun around and found him standing there in the shadows, it was that ignoring Tate Sinclair's presence was impossible.

Especially when he had his arms around her.

CHAPTER TWO

It would have been easier to pick her up and carry her out of the building, to say the heck with this crazy drama with the dress and just get her outside where she could not be embarrassed any longer. She didn't want to draw attention to herself but he doubted very seriously that they were not drawing eyes already the way they were walking, snuggled up like this. But maybe not, considering the dancing was going full swing and the lights were down low.

"Tate, Gigi. What's up?"

Tate halted, yanking Gigi even closer. Gigi

stiffened up and felt about as pliable as a two by four. "Don't panic," he muttered. "It's just my brother Jonah."

"Well, get rid of him, please," she whispered.

He looked over his shoulder. "Hey, Jonah. We're just going out to the parking lot." He snuggled Gigi a little closer to him again, if that were possible. He bent his head down and muttered into her ear, "Relax." It probably looked as if he were kissing her ear. He'd hear about that tomorrow. Not tonight. When he looked over at Jonah, he was staring at him with a grin on his face. "Don't look like that," he warned.

Gigi turned slightly to see Jonah, turning Tate with her. "Hey, Jonah."

Jonah grinned. "Hey. You two look like you're getting ready to dance."

"No, we're going to my car." Gigi smiled at Jonah.

Tate couldn't help teasing her by nudging her hair with his nose. "A dance would be good. I haven't danced since I got here." She elbowed him in the stomach. He coughed. *Why was he needling her?* She looked up at him, fire in her pretty eyes. He liked it.

"I don't want to dance," she gritted through clenched teeth.

"Come on, you got to help him out." Jonah chuckled. "Poor guy's injured foot is cramping his style."

"True." He grinned at her. "Come on—give me a dance then I'll take you to the parking lot and let you go home. Just one dance."

"How am I supposed to do that?" she whispered.

"Jonah, why aren't you dancing with Summer?"

"I'm taking her a glass of punch." He held up two glasses of punch. He looked from him to Gigi. "Sure, but…is everything okay? You two look—"

"We're fine. I'm just helping Gigi get to her car." Tate willed Jonah to take a hint and leave. Gigi was really tense.

Jonah stared at her. "Are you feeling okay?"

"I'm tired, ready to call it a night. I—"

He did not want to lie to Jonah and, anyway, he was trustworthy. "She had a little mishap back there. Don't tell anybody—she doesn't want to take any focus off Brad and Lulu."

Jonah studied how close they were standing and cocked his head slightly. "I don't exactly understand, but okay. You better get on out of here. Gigi, it was good seeing you here. You're going to have to get out from behind that counter at Bake My Day a little more often. Lately, unless somebody comes in that bakery, we don't see you around. I'm not sure why that is."

"I have things to do when I get off work. That's why. See you later, Jonah. Have fun."

She clasped his hands tight and started walking, and he went with her. They had it down now: he stepped when she stepped so their legs went at the same time. It still would've been easier if she just stood on his long feet and he walked with her on there like that, or if he picked her up and just carried her. But if he picked her up and carried her, then—well, those red panties would be shining out from underneath his arm. Everybody in the room would see them and she would probably slap him.

He kind of liked shy.

They were halfway through the crowd when he

spotted Lila Peabody hustling toward them. Right behind her was Mami Desmond. Oh boy, if those two got them cornered, he didn't figure Gigi was ever going to get out of the building. He did the only thing he knew to do in order to save Gigi from having to stand there and get bombarded with questions while trying to hide her undies—and it saved himself too. He swept her into his arms, spun her to the side so that her rear faced the door where there was barely anyone standing, and the ladies approaching wouldn't be able to get but a flash of her redness, and he headed straight toward the exit and out the door. He had barely registered her gasp and yelp as he had picked her up and walked out the door.

"What are you doing? Lila and Mami are gaping at us and I'm pretty sure they just got flashed by my red undies—" She broke off as the door slammed behind them and they were outside in the night air.

Tate was careful as he stepped from the concrete porch onto the gravel parking lot. His boot hindered him a little and slid slightly on the rock, so he concentrated on not slipping down with Gigi in his arms. "I was saving you from them. I know *exactly* what Lila and Mami do." He met her alarmed eyes, so close he could have kissed her. The thought startled him and his gaze dropped instantly to her full lips. His gut tightened and he swallowed the sudden flash of desire to kiss her.

"Um." He cleared his throat that was suddenly clogged with wants of things he did not need to be thinking. "If they're going to start rumors about us, then you being plastered all over me like this isn't going to start any less talk than me carrying you out the door will. Frankly, me being selfish, I didn't want to answer questions. So here we are, you and me alone in the parking lot. Now, which car is yours?"

He held onto her, realizing that he wasn't at all ready to let her go despite the ache intensifying in his ankle.

* * *

Gigi was having a hard time not thinking about how good it felt to be held in Tate's arms and to feel his

19

hard chest against her. "You're probably right. That's my car, the white Mustang on the end down there." She needed to get out of his arms. She needed to get out of them now.

The fact that he had swung her into his capable arms and carried her out of the reception had startled her. He'd saved her from exposing her backside to all the guests and then from endless questions from Lila and Mami. She owed him and she knew it but she'd figure out how to repay him later.

"Nice car. A '66?"

"Close—a '67. I bought it because the older man selling it wanted someone he thought would love it and take care of it, so he sold it to me for a very sweet price. I love it and baby it. Thankfully, it's still running."

"You did good, Gigi. I like it."

She needed to get out of his arms. She didn't need to be tempting herself with things that weren't good for her, and Tate Sinclair was not good for her. Anybody who felt the strong call of the world and traveled it excessively with wanderlust running through their veins was definitely not good for her. She'd already lost someone she loved to that and she didn't plan to do it again. No matter how gorgeous he was, or how strong and secure his arms felt around her.

"Okay, *now* you can put me down."

He hesitated, still holding her gently. "What if I don't want to?"

Her breath caught. "Well, that's actually not an option since I asked you to put me down."

His lips curved up and his eyes twinkled in the moonlight. "Okay, but I've kind of gotten used to holding you. Would you like to go out to eat tomorrow night?"

He was asking her out. "No, I don't think so."

Frown lines etched his face. "You're not going to eat tomorrow?"

"Yes, I'm going to eat." She made herself not give in to saying yes.

"Just not with me?"

"Right. I've already inconvenienced you enough, so you can let me down. I'll get in my car and I'll go home. And you can do whatever you came to town to do, other than come to your brother's wedding."

"Well, actually, coming to my brother's wedding was the main reason for my trip, and to get this ankle healed up." He set her on her feet. "I would like it if you go to dinner with me tomorrow."

"That's not a good idea."

"So I'm good enough to help you escape my brother's wedding but I'm not good enough to take you to dinner. That just doesn't sound quite right."

"Look, Tate, you don't want to go out with me. You're just saying that because this is an awkward situation. Honestly, you've been wonderful and thank you so much for helping me, but you don't have to keep this up."

"But I want to. And actually, if you're going to force me to play the only hand I have, then I'm going to say that you owe me dinner. You know, for saving you." He hitched a brow, as though he'd just issued a challenge.

"That's not fair and you know it. You don't want to go out to dinner with me. I don't know why you're asking me. But I guess I will. But I don't get off work until five." She was being rude and she knew it. But going out with him was dangerous to her.

"Then you tell me where to pick you up at and I'll pick you up at six-thirty. We'll have dinner and maybe do some more dancing. Since I didn't get to dance with you here tonight."

"You can't dance with that ankle."

"Watch me. Just wear something that won't rip off from slamming doors."

She fought not to laugh. "I'll try. I don't think that could happen again in a million years."

"I wouldn't get cocky if I were you. You never know. Stranger things have happened."

She laughed. "Oh, I'm not real sure of any stranger thing than my dress getting snapped up by a door could happen. But I'll be on the lookout."

"Great. And I look forward to taking you out to dinner tomorrow night."

She saw the strain in his expression now. "Then you should go home and put that leg up—rest that ankle. Or I might have to push you around in a wheelchair tomorrow."

"Nope, no wheelchair for me. I'll be fine."

"I hope you're right. But if not, I'll give you my phone number and you can call me, and I'll come rescue you anytime."

"Hey, whatever it takes to get your number sounds like something I can get behind. Give me that number and I promise I won't exploit it—I'll only use it if it's an emergency. And then you can come to my rescue." He handed her his phone.

Why had she offered him her number? "Right." She punched her number into his phone then handed it back to him. Their fingers brushed and she felt a tingle of electric connection at the touch and quickly let her hand drop to her side. She kept her back away from him, opened the door of her car and carefully angled herself down onto the black-and-white checked upholstered seat.

"You did that well." He smiled.

Butterflies fluttered in her chest. She swung her legs in and cranked the engine. It purred like a cat.

At the sound, Tate's expression brightened. "Sounds sweet. You'll have to take me riding."

"I guess I can take you tomorrow." *What?*

"Now that sounds like a date. Tomorrow—I'll see you then." He closed the door and stepped back, smiling as he watched her back out of the parking space.

She had agreed to a date with the man who had been the object of her affection. An unattainable dream…she needed to remember that he was still just as unattainable.

CHAPTER THREE

Gigi was swamped the next morning at the bakery because Rosie called in sick again. She had been fighting morning sickness ever since learning she and Adam were expecting the first Sinclair grandchild.

Gigi felt bad for her friend and boss, but she knew Rosie would make it through, and Rosie wouldn't trade being pregnant for anything in the world. Gigi had assured her that everything was fine and that she could handle it and didn't mind at all coming in for the early shift. Normally Rosie was the one who did all the morning baking, coming in at five in the morning. Gigi had offered many times to give her a break but Rosie loved that time of the morning and, until now, had always done the first baking of the day herself. Hopefully, when she got through these first few months, Rosie would start feeling better. Gigi hoped for her friend's sake that was the way it would be. However, she understood some women could have morning sickness the whole time. She really hoped this wasn't Rosie's case. Ever the positive person, Rosie would never let it be known how bad she felt. At the wedding, she had looked beautiful, though she was a little bit pale, and Adam had really watched over her carefully. One of the benefits of being married to a doctor was that she got first-rate care.

By seven-thirty, the new hire arrived to help. Gigi had started off as part-time help, then moved into the full-time position when Rosie had realized two part-time helpers weren't going to work. Now, they had a high school student, Kelly, who came in after school to help and Trena, who had been with them for a while, helped her through the mornings during the main morning coffee and muffin rush.

They were busy. It was as if on Monday mornings, everyone had to get their Bake My Day muffin fix. It was the busiest morning in all of the week. By mid-morning, about the time the rush started easing up, the four ladies she'd known would drop in entered the bakery. Lila, Mami, Birdie, and Doreen walked in with wide grins on their faces. The group never ceased to make her smile, with their affectionate meddling ways of trying to bring people together. But she had never been the object of their misguided affection. She and Tate were not—never would be—a couple. It was out of the question on so many levels. But she could tell from their expressions that convincing them of this might be impossible.

All of them had excited and expectant looks on their faces: Lila, with her stylish blonde bob haircut and lively, knowing eyes that had a I-can't-be-fooled glow to them. Mami, the robust, fun-loving romantic, had seen Tate swing her into his arms. With her height, not much got by her. Lila was shorter and might have missed a few details—like the probability that someone had gotten flashed by her red undies as he scooped her up. But not Mami. And the twinkle of her alert eyes told Gigi she'd seen everything and thought it was a perfect meet-cute like in the old romantic comedy movies—girl's dress gets halfway ripped off and cute hero rescues her—yep, it had the makings of legendary beginnings.

Birdie, on the other hand, was tiny like a bird, with a crinkled face and a blunt way of stating things. Doreen was short in stature, well-endowed—or top-heavy, as she put it most of the time—but shy as they came. She just looked tickled pink, and her sweet gaze watched with expectation as they all marched up to the counter.

Blunt Birdie spoke first. "Had yourself a hunk of a date at the wedding, I see."

Gigi tried to keep her expression neutral. "No date for me," she said, feeling every bit ready to run and hide in the back room.

Lila grinned. "I saw you at the wedding and you looked positively smitten with that gorgeous Tate Sinclair. We never even knew you and he had a thing."

"How have you kept that quiet?" Mami gave her

the you-been-keeping-a-secret look. "I declare, I was totally startled when I spotted you two cuddled up together. And then he swept you into his arms, all *Gone-with-the-Wind* like…you looked positively in love."

"Now, ladies, hold on—it wasn't what it looked like."

Birdie harrumphed. "I don't see how you can deny that when I saw him sweep you up into his arms. I was across the room from Mami and Lila, but I saw exactly what they saw except I was closer to the door and saw him carry you outside."

Doreen had pink cheeks. "It was very romantic. I could barely see y'all over everybody's heads, since I'm so short. I had to, like, push my way past a few people to see what in the world was going on. I'll tell you, it was so romantic seeing him walk out the door, holding you like that." Doreen sighed and placed a hand to her large bosom. "It's just *sooo* romantic."

Gigi was speechless as her gaze darted from one lady to the other.

"Gigi, you're just too quiet," Lila declared. "All

this time, everybody's been having these romances and Tate's been coming to town and we didn't even notice the two of you connecting."

"It's like y'all been hiding under the radar," Birdie finished.

This was getting out of hand. "Now, ladies, honestly, it's not like that. There was no radar. We haven't been seeing each other."

Four sets of disbelieving eyes blinked at her. They all looked at her as if they had her number and she couldn't lie to them.

Lila waved her hand. "Say what you want to, dear. But we know our stuff and we can tell when someone's trying to hoodwink us. You and Tate Sinclair have been having a romance right under our noses. While we've all been encouraging these other romances along, you two have been able to sneak around and hide it from us. How could we have missed it?"

Mami dropped her chin to her chest and huffed, "I have no idea." She pulled her jaw back in place. "I saw him come in here once and I saw him look at you and you looked at him…and y'all were very good actors because I never ever suspected there was a romance going on between you two love birds."

Oh, for heaven's sake. Gigi rubbed her now throbbing temple. "There isn't a romance going on, ladies. Come on. I work here and last night Tate helped me out of a…a situation." She really didn't want to tell everybody about her embarrassing situation.

Mami eyed her very closely. "Now, Gigi, come on, girl. You deserve love just as much as everybody else. There's nothing to be embarrassed about. I have to tell you, I never suspected it because, well, Tate, with all of his wanderings and all of his things that he does, he just didn't seem like your type. You're such a homebody. I never envisioned that the two of you would be a couple. How are you going to handle that when he goes off?"

"I'm handling it quite well because there isn't anything going on, so when he leaves it's no big deal." Thankfully, the door opened and a group of unfamiliar faces entered. She had never been so glad to see a group of tourists in all of her life! "Ooops—getting busy. Go on over and have a seat and if you want something different than your regular order, just let me know. If not, I'll bring your regulars in just a few minutes."

Mami grinned. "I'll take my regular. And we're going to go over here and wait till you have time to sit down and chat a while. We need to figure out a way to help our Rosie and her morning sickness, and help you figure out how you two will maintain a marriage logistically."

No way—she hadn't gone *there*.

They weren't even dating…well, not technically…and now they were getting *married*.

Oh brother.

She had agreed to go out with Tate tonight but as far as she was concerned, that was going to be a secret because if anyone got wind of that, this nonsense would only get worse. She would make sure they went somewhere that nobody would recognize them. Down the coast would work. Somewhere there were plenty of places to eat where they wouldn't run into anybody from Sunset Bay.

* * *

Tate picked Gigi up at her house on the outskirts of town. It was a very small bungalow that was at the end of an older neighborhood. From her yard, she had a small view of the ocean because her house stuck out on a small inlet to the ocean. He had a feeling the neighborhood was probably owned by long-term residents.

Her place was homey, with teal-blue paint and white shutters, a little *Welcome* beach sign in the flower bed, and colorful potted plants. On the side of the house was a cute sitting area with teal-blue Adirondack chairs that faced the small sliver of ocean that could be seen.

The door opened and he turned from studying the yard to see Gigi. He almost bit his tongue off at the vision she made. Standing in the doorway in a black dress that showed off her curves—because Gigi had curves—her dark hair hung across her shoulders, accentuating her sweet face and large eyes.

She took his breath away. He swallowed hard and

took a step forward, forgetting about his injured ankle and stepping too fast so that he paid for it, grimacing as he slowed.

"Careful, don't hurt yourself."

"Yeah, I'll be glad when I don't have to worry about this." He reached her and placed a hand on the porch post to take the weight off his ankle for a minute. He smiled. "May I say that you are a vision?"

She blushed. "Don't get carried away. I just threw this old thing on."

He laughed. "Yeah, well, you did a really good job throwing it on. Anyway, you ready to go? I like your place. Might have to come back and sit in that cute little red chair with you sometime."

She put her hand on her hip and cocked her head to the side. "I don't know that that's going to be a good idea or an option. I'm just going to dinner with you."

"You are stubborn, but we'll get back to that later. What are you hungry for? I thought we might go to that Italian restaurant by the pier. It's great."

"Actually, there's a new place near Fort Myers and I'd really like to try that out."

"We can go out of town. If that's what you want."

She didn't want to be seen with him. If she thought he didn't know what she was doing, then she was wrong. But he didn't care; he'd go either way.

"That's what I want. I'm going out with you to pay you back for rescuing me. And a date seems the perfect time to try out the new restaurant."

"Sounds good to me." He watched her as she strode toward his truck, her black skirt flouncing as she walked. He smiled and decided he'd go anywhere with her. He was just moving slower because he was still paying the price for having carried her the night before, but he wasn't complaining.

CHAPTER FOUR

They managed to make it through small talk on the drive to the seaside restaurant and he had to admit, as they were seated near a window of the fairly elegant restaurant, that she had chosen well. "I have to admit, you had a very good idea. This looks very interesting. Thank you for coming up with this idea."

After the waitress left with their orders, he settled back to enjoy himself. "Did you get a lot of flak about the episode after the wedding? Mami and her group—did they come to the bakery and wonder why in the world I had swept you out of there like that?"

She looked less than enthusiastic. "They think you and I have a little thing going on. I tried to set them straight. But, oh no, they don't want to hear that, so they're probably going to start sneaking around, trying to fix us up. Or at the least bugging us to death."

"I'm afraid you're right."

"Oh, I know I'm right. But I'm not one to be manipulated." She bit her lip. A look of worry shadowed her pretty face. Then her eyes narrowed. "It's just I'd hoped to stay under their radar. I'm not excited about being asked every time I see them about how we're doing."

He laid a hand across his heart. "I'm so hurt. Just like that, you've made your decision that you're not going to go out with me or let them enjoy watching our romance blossom. What have I done to make you make that snap judgment like that? Can you enlighten me about what you have against me?"

She stared at him, her mouth slack. He held her gaze, waiting.

She sighed. "Okay, so here's the deal. I don't date guys who don't stick around. To be honest, I've done

38

that. I've bought that line and I've had to nurse a broken heart because of it. And I'm not ever going to do that again."

His stomach sank. *She had been hurt.* He should have picked up on that already. "Some guy broke your heart and you're judging me because of that?"

"Some *guy* broke my heart because I didn't pay attention to the warning signs. That is never happening again because I'm not ever missing warning signs ever again. And men with wanderlust in their veins are off-limits."

Men like him, she was saying. "What did this dude do to you?"

She sighed. "Moved to Fort Myers where I was working, won my heart, then decided adventure overseas was a better option after all and moved on. He said he was ready to settle down and I believed him…" She looked out the window at the ocean.

Tate studied her profile. His heart hurt for her. She looked back at him and her eyes glittered with bitterness.

"He said that during the eight months that he was

here that he was happy and ready to settle down. Then he got a call for a job offer in Switzerland, of all places, and the call of the Alps and extreme snowboarding and all kinds of exciting adventures were just too big of a pull for him to say no. The next thing I know, he had his plane ticket and a duffel bag packed, kissed me on the cheek, told me he was sorry and then he was gone. Just like that, in the blink of an eye. Wanderlust is not my friend. So, you see, Tate, nothing against you. You're really a nice guy. You came to my rescue last night and I really appreciate it. But that's all there is. I don't date anymore. I'm happy with my life like it is. There is a lot to be said about contentment."

"You don't date at all?"

"No. I'm not interested. I work."

She wasn't interested in dating? "Why?"

"I'm busy."

"Working at the bakery. I guess you enjoy that?"

"Yes. Do you have a problem with that?"

She was prickly. "No. Just curious."

"I waitressed while I took college classes and

almost got an accounting degree. I met Bill during that time and after he left me for his adventures, I zoned out for a while and I haven't gone back."

"Really?"

"Yes, I moved back here, got a job at the bakery and love it. My evenings are free and I don't have any huge responsibility. And I don't date."

"I get the no dating for now. But, I'm still confused—it's real important to you not to have any responsibility?" Their drinks came and the waitress smiled as she set his in front of him. He gave her a quick smile and didn't really meet her eyes as he looked back at his date.

"Yes. I know you must think I'm a lazy-bones or not very ambitious."

"I didn't say that." He studied her, his gaze narrowing. "Nope, just doesn't fit at all. What do you do in your spare time? Do you garden? Read a lot? Watch tons of television?"

She leaned back in her seat and crossed her arms, giving him a sarcastic glare. "He doth judge me."

"No," he said quickly. "I'm just saying you seem

like a fairly energetic person or you wouldn't work at that busy bakery. I just can't see you going home and doing nothing—okay, forget what I'm saying. I've completely talked myself into a corner."

"Yes, you have…" She toyed with her napkin, and he could see she was thinking hard about something. She bit her lip and met his gaze.

"What?"

"I write. I'm kind of obsessed with it. But it doesn't pay the bills, so I work at the bakery."

He hadn't seen that coming. "A writer? Really?"

"Yes really, you don't have to be so surprised. I don't need much to be content, so the bakery job gets me out of the house…keeps me from being a hermit. And I love seeing people, so it's perfect."

"So, what do you write?"

She sat straighter. "I write romantic suspense."

Again, he hadn't expected that. "So, I don't want to ask the obvious question but you said they don't pay the bills—have you published them? I mean, have they been bought?"

"No. They haven't. And that question is the reason

I don't tell anyone about what I do."

His smile widened. "It's okay. If I've learned anything, it's keep pushing for your dreams. Keep submitting and it will happen. I'm rooting for you."

She looked nervous as she toyed with her napkin.

"Thanks. I have an entire six-book series written but I do it for my own enjoyment. I haven't submitted them to anyone." She said the last part of the sentence really fast.

"Did you say you haven't sent them out yet?"

She nodded.

He looked confused. "But—how long have you been writing them?"

"A few years. Five." She squeaked out the last word.

He coughed. "You have been writing them for five years and you haven't *ever* sent them out to see if someone would publish them?"

"No, I sent the first one out once…an-and, you know, right after I started, they told me that they only took agented manuscripts. So, I tried to get an agent. And he rejected me. Then the next one charged me a lot of money to edit the book and get it ready for the publishers and then it never sold. I don't have to be published. I enjoy writing the books. That's all I need, so I stopped submitting."

He knew he was about to tread on really shaky ground. "Did somebody scam you? Or is that a legitimate way—that an editor takes all your money and then doesn't try to sell it or doesn't sell it? Not that I know anything about what I'm talking about, I'm just asking."

She studied her plate, then looked out at the water and then looked back at him. "Okay, so I got scammed. Yes, some legitimate agents do charge to rehabilitate or whatever they call getting a manuscript ready if they think that they can sell it. And there are no guarantees that it will sell. Then there are others who make a living off scamming people who want to sell their work. You know, the problem with people who want to be an author—sometimes they want it so bad that their perspective gets blurry. And that's what happened to me. My gut told me not to send them the chunk of money but I did it anyway. I learned a big lesson and now I just write for myself." She frowned, rubbed her forehead and then glared at him. "Now I told you my secret—are you happy? So don't judge me and don't try to talk me into submitting my work. And please don't tell anybody this. I don't know why I told you in the first place. Nobody knows that story."

Fury coiled in his chest at the idea of anyone being scammed. But Gigi being scammed—for some reason, it seemed personal. Before he could calm down enough to speak without blowing up, she continued.

"I'm good just where I am." She rubbed the condensation on her glass. "And back to the original reason for this whole conversation—I like being at home and holing up in the evenings and the weekends, working on my books when I'm not volunteering for something around town. It gives me pleasure. I'm content. And I don't need you or anybody else telling me that I'm not. And I certainly don't need an agent or a publisher sowing discontent in my soul."

He decided that the best thing he could do right now was take a drink of his tea. And that's exactly what he did. He tried to think of something to say that wouldn't get him in trouble. If there was one thing about him, it was he never had any quit inside him. Nobody was going to tell him to quit, nobody was going to diminish his dream, nobody was going to make him stop doing what he wanted. But looking at Gigi, he knew without a doubt that she wanted her work published, but she had hidden her dream because somebody had messed her around.

But instead of pushing through it and going for her dream anyway, she'd retreated and now lived the lie that it was fine.

The truth was, he and Gigi were complete opposites.

Were they even compatible?

CHAPTER FIVE

Why had she spilled her guts to Tate Sinclair?

Gigi asked herself this the next evening as she paced the little flagstone sitting area back and forth, past the fire pit that sat in front of the two Adirondack chairs. Normally this was her relaxing place in the evenings. She spent a lot of evenings sitting here with her laptop, writing, or with a yellow legal pad, plotting her books. Not today. Today, she had Tate on her mind. She had been reliving their evening together ever since he'd dropped her off at her door last night.

She'd been distracted at work but thankfully it had

been so busy, she hadn't had time to visit with anyone who'd come in other than to take their orders and give them a smile. And thankfully, he hadn't come by. Why would he? He hadn't said anything about her writing for the rest of the dinner or ride home. Just as she'd asked.

Why had she confessed to him that she had let someone take advantage of her? The very thought that she'd had that happen to her was so embarrassing. She knew that people got scammed every day and it was terrible. But it had happened to her and she hadn't ever told anyone. Maybe she should have. If she'd told someone close to her, she could have maybe helped someone else not get scammed by the same person.

The thought tugged at her. And she knew just by the look of total fury that crossed Tate's eyes that he hadn't liked the idea of her being scammed. He probably wouldn't like anyone being scammed, so she didn't let herself get excited about the fact—his emotion was not personal. Nor had she wanted it to be, she reminded herself.

Then there was the total disbelief on his face when

she'd admitted she'd never sent her work in again. That *had* been personal. Tate didn't understand her. She knew a man like him would think that was ridiculous. She appeared very straightforward; most people took her at face value. She was sometimes pretty blunt and take-charge and, well, everyone just assumed that that was exactly her personality when it was, in many ways, a lie. Pulling back the curtain and exposing her innermost feelings anymore was something she couldn't do.

Writing, sending her work out, and letting someone tell her how terrible it was again was too personal. She understood it went back to the pain of rejection when her father had abandoned her and her mother. She'd been terrified of anyone learning the truth of her and her mother's situation those last couple of years here in Sunset Bay. She'd felt so vulnerable during that time and she'd built up walls to hide behind.

Sending her work out those few times she'd done it had taken a huge effort on her part. She'd felt exposed and vulnerable, and she'd been taken advantage of and rejected.

She couldn't do that again.

Glancing back at her computer on the small table between the two teal-colored chairs, she sat down and pulled it into her lap. She stared at the open screen and the story that she had been working on for a month now. It was a good story and she was enjoying it. It *was* good. She sighed. *What if she tried to send in or just tried that self-publishing avenue?*

She listened to a lot of podcasts and YouTube videos on how to self-publish. She had been to each of the retailer's sites and looked into how to do it. Her pulse raced at the thought. It would be putting it out there and people could read it. She just wasn't sure. If it was really good enough, she should just send it to more agents and see whether any of them would represent her— *No. Who was she kidding?* She was comfortable and content sitting here, doing it her own way.

She rubbed her forehead. See, *that's* why she shouldn't have gone out with Tate Sinclair. The overachiever that he was of course would think that someone who didn't take a chance, didn't risk something or push hard enough—yes, he would think they were giving up, that they were a loser. So why had she told him all of her secrets?

All about her ex dropping her then her writing— Tate probably went home thinking she was just a big bundle of joy and a loser.

She sighed. It was probably for the best. They were complete opposites of each other. She had just grown content with things the way they were. Why was she going to let this guy come in and make her second-guess herself? Make her think about things that she had pushed to the back of her mind and heart a long time ago? She did not need anything more than what she had now. She was very grateful for her friends, her wonderful job, and this beautiful town. She didn't need anything else.

She stared at the words she had written and then, her fingers back on the keys, she began to type. This was why she wrote. The sheer wonder of her fingers tapping away, creating a story, just thrilled her. She didn't need anybody's pat on the back to feel good about her novel.

And she needed to get over this rekindled infatuation with Tate. It was better that he find out now that they were complete opposites. Maybe he wouldn't ask her out again.

If he stayed away from her, it would be easier for her to stay away from him.

* * *

Bake My Day was closed on Sunday, but just as Gigi had suspected, Rosie called that afternoon and asked her to open on Monday morning. Then, on Monday morning, after Gigi had gotten the first rush of customers taken care of, she'd called again. Gigi had let Trena take care of the front counter as she went to the storeroom for the call.

"Is everything all right?" she asked, worried about Rosie but trying not to let on how much. She knew Rosie had had serious health issues prior to moving to Sunset Bay.

"Gigi, I'm so sorry. I should have told you this

yesterday. I decided to stop kidding myself. I'm going to probably be on leave for a while. Get Trena to come in as many hours as you need her or as she can. If you need to hire someone else, then do it. I'm not going to be able to make it in the rest of this week. And I might not be able to make it in next week. Adam and my obstetrician agreed, talking this morning, that my system was so compromised by my cancer, when I was so sick a few years ago, that me having a baby is a miracle. The fact is, I have to take precautions and that means staying off my feet as much as possible."

Gigi's heart clutched in her chest and her thoughts flew to the baby. "Rosie, the baby is okay, right? You're all right?"

Over the phone, she couldn't see Rosie's face but there was a pause, and it had Gigi very worried. This baby was so special to this entire family. Gigi knew how much Rosie and Adam wanted the baby and she knew how much Maryetta, Adam and Tate's mother, wanted a grandchild. The poor woman was having baby cravings so badly that she was driving her entire family crazy. She was already buying baby clothes and the baby was not even three months conceived. This was hard.

"The baby is fine. We're just being cautious. Right now, thank goodness, it's more me, with the dizziness and the weakness I'm experiencing. It's all going to be great. Really."

Gigi wasn't completely sure that she believed it was that simple but Rosie was always optimistic. It was part of her DNA and though she didn't talk about her illness very much, Gigi knew that she had almost died at one point. Gigi wasn't sure how many other people in town knew that she had been so ill before moving to Sunset Bay because even Gigi had just happened to overhear Adam and Rosie talking one day about it.

She felt very certain that Rosie didn't tell everyone because she was very much an it's-not-about-me-but-about-you person. Rosie was all about lifting others up, but Gigi knew everyone wanted to be there for her.

"Rosie, I'm here and I will do whatever I need to run this business like you do. That's my job now. Your job is to relax, rest, do whatever the baby doctor tells you to do or that gorgeous doctor husband of yours tells you. Making this sweet baby comfortable is top priority. So if you have to stay in bed for the next six months and I have to run this place, I will do that. And I will do it with a smile. I'll try very hard to be as optimistic as you are, but you know that's pretty much impossible because you are amazing."

Rosie laughed gently. The joyous sound made Gigi smile even over the phone line.

"I'll do that," Rosie said. "And, Gigi, you know good and well that you make everyone smile who comes into Bake My Day. Especially me, because I know that you're the best and I can rely completely on you. And that gives me great comfort. I have to warn you that I will do whatever I need to do to keep my sweet baby safe and that might mean I have to rely on you for the next six months, and even after the baby comes. I'm probably going to want to stay home more, but I can promise you I'm not going to stay home all of the time. What I'm saying is I might stay home some and share management with you."

Gigi took in what Rosie had just said. "Are you telling me that I'm not just going to be helping out while you're sick? That I'm actually managing?" This was telling because this meant Rosie really was stepping back some. Was there more to the story than she knew? Maybe Rosie was being very optimistic when really there was more danger for the baby than she was letting on. Or even for Rosie. Gigi's mind careened out of control with worry. She loved Rosie. Rosie had come into town at a time when Gigi desperately needed a new job and something positive to take her mind off having lost her boyfriend, Bill, whom she had thought was going to be her husband.

"Yes."

Swallowing down her fear, she forced herself not to sound worried. "Again, I'll do whatever you want me to do. Now, do you want me to bake your famous muffins and bring them by to you to taste every morning? Because I'll do that—you know, you're going to need something to sustain you." She smiled when Rosie giggled again. The sound just made her happy.

"I'm not going to make you bring me muffins but I will make some of my brothers-in-law or my husband stop by and bring them to me. Or I might even make my sister-in-law come by and get them. You know, I'm very blessed for someone who didn't have a lot of close people in my life for a while. Now I've got them everywhere. It's truly wonderful."

"I hear ya, sister. So, all right, we're prepared. Now, I better get to managing this place because I have a very strict boss and I wouldn't want to disappoint her. And I see some very demanding clientele coming through the door right now."

"Oh my. Is it Lila and the girls?"

"Yes. And you know they're giving me a hard time because of what Tate did at the wedding, sweeping me off my feet and carrying me outside. They think that we're an item, so they're probably going to give me the fourth degree again—or the ninth degree. They're going to drill questions through me again like they did the other day. There's no convincing them that it's not true."

"I'm not totally convinced either. Come on,

Gigi—he's gorgeous, he's in town, and I, for one, think that you and him would make a great couple. So, relax and maybe take a hint…if I were you, I'd get a date with him. You know, bat those pretty eyes at him. Or go by his place and take him a few muffins."

"Rosie, I don't need the girls *and* you after me."

"Okay, okay. But I'm just saying…" She giggled and then the line went dead.

Heaving a resigned sigh, Gigi moved from the storeroom to the counter. Trena was busy and that left her facing four pairs of overly excited eyes.

"Hello, ladies. I hope you're having a good morning."

Mami plopped one bejeweled hand on the top of the muffin showcase and leaned toward Gigi. "Have you seen our gorgeous world traveler anymore this week?"

Gigi forced a laugh and prayed her face didn't give away the fact that, yes, she had seen him. "I have not." She crossed her fingers behind her back because of the little white lie that she was telling. Yes, it was wrong and she felt guilty, but it was either that or have them practically marry her off before they left the shop.

Lila put her fist on her hips. "Do you mean Tate hasn't been by here? You'd think when a man sweeps a woman off her feet he'd at least come by and talk to her. Or at least use getting a muffin as an excuse to see you. It's just not making sense. He's had several days since we last saw you."

Birdie, about the size of a stork and with some perpetual frown lines on her sun-wrinkled face, scrunched her tight lips to one side and got a thoughtful gleam in her eyes. "I know we didn't misread something the other day. That boy flipped you off your feet as if y'all were in *Gone with the Wind*. Could've been carrying you up a set of big long stairs the way he swept you out of that place. Did you do something to make him mad?"

Why would they automatically think she had done something? "Ladies, Birdie, come on—it's not like that. I've told you all there is nothing between us. Now, I'll get your coffee ready while all of you go sit down and talk. I'll bring your regulars."

Taking a hint, Doreen, bless her heart, turned to her friends. "Come on y'all, let's leave her alone. She's going to bring our coffee and muffins over. And besides, I see a crowd coming this way. We better let her get our order or it's going to take forever."

Thankfully the ladies listened and headed to the window table they frequented several days of the week. Gigi hurried about getting their usual muffin orders ready: strawberry cream cheese delight for two of them and then cinnamon orange marmalade for the other two.

People were waiting at the counter after she dropped them off at the table, along with their coffee orders, so she had that excuse not to hang around for more of their interrogation. She was very thankful that the place got very busy—it saved her from answering any more questions.

Questions she didn't want to answer or think about. She'd been thinking about him constantly and the one thing she knew was the hunk of good-looking, wandering stuntman, Tate Sinclair would not get off her mind. Nor would he be good for her.

She kept telling herself that nothing good would come out of her having this infatuation with him. It hadn't when she had been in school and it wouldn't now. He would leave just like Bill had, because Tate loved adventure so very much. Craved it as much as she craved small-town life and security. She had decided already that if she ever started dating again—if she could be that brave—she would seek only someone safe.

So why did she continue to have Tate Sinclair on her mind?

They were complete opposites of each other, she reminded herself over and over again. He was a risk-taker in everything he was involved in and she wasn't.

Nope, she had a job to do; she had to make Rosie proud. She had to keep this wonderful little bakery going and she had to stay optimistic if she was going to do this job as well as Rosie.

Because that would be her way of showing Rosie that she cared for her and she could count on her. That was one thing Gigi did well: letting people know they could count on her.

She hadn't always been able to do that in her young life growing up and she certainly hadn't been able to do it with her love life. But people could count on her.

And that was the way it would always be.

CHAPTER SIX

Tate stood on the deck of his rented bungalow and watched the early morning waves roll in. He had been home over a week now and it was killing him that he couldn't be jogging down that beach like he normally would. This having to tend to his injured ankle was getting to him. He heard a knock on his door; it opened and then he heard Adam call out to him.

"I'm out here," he called and then, in a minute, his brother walked out onto the deck. "How are you, Doc?" He grinned.

Adam had been a high-energy trauma doctor and now he was a small-town doctor living a slower pace and with a baby on board. It was hard to wrap his head around sometimes—from the frenzied pace of his career in some of the largest trauma units in the country to now, being known as "Doc" in slow-paced Sunset Bay.

"I'm fine. How's the patient?"

"Getting very impatient." Tate sank into the deck chair, lifted his boot to the table in front of him, and waved a hand toward the foot. "When are you going to spring me from this thing?"

"I'm going to check it out here in just a second and we're going to see how you're healing. The bruise to your bone from the pressure of that car crushing against your ankle and tendons is not going to heal as quickly as you hope. A bone bruise is not something to laugh about. Mixed with a sprain, it takes a little while. A break would've been easier."

"Great. Just what I want to hear. You see that water out there? You see that beautiful white sand? You know what I want to be doing right now."

Adam sat down in the chair across from him and started unstrapping the boot on Tate's foot.

House calls were nice when you had a doctor in the family. He didn't like going into the clinic, having everybody look at him and knowing he was injured. It was pretty silly on his part but still, it was nice that Adam dropped by to check on his ankle.

He leveled a serious gaze on him. "In time, you'll be able to do that. But honestly, I know you…if I take that boot off too soon, you'll be on it before you need to be. You'll probably be off doing some kind of crazy thing or you might go back to that ill-fated movie set and attempt to do that stunt over again. They aren't calling you, are they?"

They had called him to see whether he could get back to try it again, but he hadn't wanted to admit that to his brother. It would just make him and his family worry. He had told them to give up the stunt and do something safer because he wouldn't be back to do it, and he didn't want somebody else getting hurt. Already, two of the best stuntmen in the industry, him being one of the two, getting hurt on something was probably going to be hard on their budget. They might as well back off and do something different.

"They called but I turned them down." He decided he better be honest.

"Well, that's good. But still, if I take that boot off too soon, you'll be doing something crazy. Even jogging down that soft sand is off-limits for now. You need to take it easy. This ankle needs to last you for the rest of your life and if you want it to do what you need it to do, then you need to take care of it right now. It's kind of like Rosie. She's energetic and, you know, a do-gooder. She wants to be out there at her shop, greeting everybody and making them all feel wonderful. But she's having to stay in bed right now and take care of our baby. She is not griping about it because she knows how important it is that she does this for our baby. So, take a page from my sweet wife and do what you have to do and think positive about it. Relax, go easy on your ankle, and do what you can to enjoy it while you're here."

"Fine. I'll do my best. How is Rosie?"

"Just like I told you—she's optimistic, willing to

do whatever it takes, and she and the baby are going to be just fine. It's going to be fine."

He heard the worry in his brother's voice but he didn't push. "Okay, but I'm here, so anything I can do, you let me know. Anything I can do to help her while you're working? I'm just sitting around and even though I don't move as fast as I need to, I can still get around—maybe run errands for her. I can check on her when you're too busy to do so. Anything you need, I'm your man. Jonah's got his business and Erin's got hers. I know Mom and Dad will be popping in and out. Brad's on his honeymoon—I guess they're going to be back, what, Monday or Sunday? Anyway, I'm here. I'm bored—I'm your man."

Adam looked at him, a light in his eye. "Well, Rosie did tell me there was something I could ask you to start doing."

"Anything. Whatever she needs, I'll do."

"She's having cravings for fresh muffins in the morning. She thought maybe you could go by her shop every morning, pick her up a warm muffin and a cup of coffee, and drop it by the house." Adam went to

67

looking at his ankle as if it were broken and needed extra special attention.

Tate was not fooled. He had just been set up. But how could he turn this down?

"Sure, I can do that. She can just let me know what kind she wants and I'll pick it up. I guess Gigi will be there, baking?" He flinched when Adam poked a spot on his swollen ankle.

"Yup, she'll be there. And Rosie said just have her give you whatever she wants her to have that day." Adam's lip twitched.

Tate pinned him with a I-know-what's-going-on stare.

Yep, he was being set up. "Sounds like a plan. I'll pick it up first thing in the morning. Please assure Rosie that I have everything under control."

But did he? Try as he might, he hadn't been able to get Gigi off his mind ever since dropping her off at her house after their date.

Clearly, she had said more to him than she'd been comfortable saying. All the way home, he'd known she was regretting telling him about her writing and Bill running off on her.

He had a feeling she would not be happy to see him walk into the bakery.

* * *

The next morning, Tate entered the bakery. It was not quite seven and he realized as the door closed behind him that the lights weren't on yet. It was very quiet.

"Hello. Gigi," he called. He was an early riser and had assumed the bakery would be open, though he hadn't known for sure because he had never been to the bakery early in the morning. He was an early morning jogger, not a muffin eater. No one answered him, so he took a step into the shadowy area. The lights in the area behind the counter were on but nobody was there.

Odd. The door had been unlocked, so he took another step forward. His booted foot clacked on the tile floor while his boat-shoed foot made no sound. As he neared the counter, he heard a muttering. It came from the back room. Quickly as he could, he moved around the corner of the counter and walked toward the door, past the coffeemakers and the donut trays and the muffin trays. He peeked in, not sure what he would find. He heard the mutter again. It sounded like Gigi muttering something under her breath. "Gigi," he said, then he saw her—or what appeared to be her. He saw legs hanging over a chest freezer and a shapely bottom sticking up.

He yanked his attention off her bottom and moved forward. "Gigi, are you okay?"

She yelped, jumped, and he heard her head slam into something.

"Ouch!" She reared up and hit her head on a shelf full of pots. It shook and then all the pots crashed to the floor. One was shattered into a million pieces, all on top of Gigi and knocking her back down.

He quickly moved forward. "Here, let me help." He started to pull trays off her.

She growled beneath it all. "What are you doing? You scared the living daylights out of me," she declared as he finally reached her body.

He grabbed her by the hips and gently pulled her

back, then reached for her arm and pulled her torso from where she'd been dangling. She glared at him and rubbed her head once he had her sitting up.

Her glittering eyes snapped with accusation. "What are you doing?"

"Saving you. Again. Looked like you were stuck and muttering to yourself. I couldn't understand but it looked like you were in a bind."

She huffed out an exasperated breath. "Mad is what I am."

"About what? And how is your head? Is it bruised? Can you think straight? And all that stuff fell on you—you're probably going to have bruises all over your body."

"I'm fine. It wasn't all that heavy. This freezer is not working and I was trying to see if I could get the plug jiggled enough to see if that was the problem. It's stuck. And I got myself crammed down in there and my shirt stuck on a part of the freezer. Then you scared me to death and I jumped and ripped the shirt sleeve unsticking it." She glanced down at her pretty pink shirt that now had a rip along the elbow and to the

71

wrist area.

He grimaced. "Sorry about that. But as long as you're okay, that's the most important thing. Maybe I can check out the freezer for you."

"So you're an electrician too?"

He grinned. "I'm not an electrician but I know how things work. Can't be in my business and not understand some of that. It helps me not get hurt. Or it should have, didn't work this time around."

She crossed her arms, not moving. "I never thought about that. I thought others took care of that stuff."

"They do, but I make it my business to check things, and I help come up with the stunts so I have to know how things are going to work in the stunt. Explosives aren't something to take for granted."

"Explosives? Oh gosh…that's how you got hurt? I didn't think that as a stuntman you dealt with that kind of thing."

"That and a few other things. Anyway, let me see if I can figure this out for you. If I can't fix it, we'll call you in a real electrician. How's that sound?"

"Great. I'm glad you came by—why are you here? I don't open until seven-thirty."

"I'm here to pick up muffins for Rosie."

She balked. Her shocked expression slid into resignation. "I see. I'll have to have a little talk with my boss."

"What—trying to get me fired? I don't have anything to do. I'm usually jogging right now and with this foot, I'm twiddling my thumbs and drinking coffee. At least coming by to pick up Rosie's muffins and coffee is giving me an out and an excuse to get my own Bake My Day cup of coffee."

She smiled, and it dazzled him. "You can also have a muffin on the house for doing this for Rosie."

"I'll pass on the muffin. Without jogging, if I start eating those muffins, I probably won't stop eating them and that won't be good for my business."

"Wow, so you're strictly doing this to help out Rosie? Not for the muffins? What a selfless act of kindness." She smiled, teasing.

He smiled back at her. "Oh, I definitely have an ulterior motive—seeing you."

Her smile disappeared. "Did you forget our conversation the other night? I'm not interested in you."

"Maybe if you see me as a nice guy, I might change your mind."

Her brows crinkled. "No. You won't."

"Wow, you don't hold back. Okay, I'm strictly here to help out my sister-in-law, who's having a rough time carrying a baby. You can't fault me for that. And you can't take my newfound job away. And clearly you need my services this morning. Now, move out of the way and let me look at this. I didn't see a whole lot going on out there. Do you have muffins made?"

"Don't you smell them? They're in the oven." A timer chimed. "Time to take them out of the oven. You work on that and I'll go do my business."

"You're bossy. I like it." He laughed as she shot him a glare then spun and hurried to the front. He watched her as she reached the oven.

She glanced back at him and caught him staring at her. "And while you're at it, clean up that mess, won't you?"

He laughed. "Yes, ma'am. I'll do that."

One thing was certain—he wasn't bored this morning.

* * *

The man had appeared out of nowhere.

Gigi yanked open the oven door, fighting frustration with herself for having had such a reaction to the guy. Just the sound of his voice had sent ripples of delight through her. After initially nearly scaring her to death, sneaking up on her like he had. Not that he would call it sneaking up on her considering he said he had called her name. She must have left the door unlocked instead of locking it back like she normally would. Her brain had been preoccupied this morning. On him.

And then on the freezer when she'd realized it wasn't working. She had been prepared to call an electrician then got hung up. They had a walk-in freezer but it was full of all their supplies; this was the freezer they stored their muffins in to freeze quickly before shipment. It was a new endeavor they had been attempting to get off the ground. It was a delicate situation because the muffins had to be frozen just right, and then they had to be placed in with the right amount of dry ice and mailed out. She did not want to mess this up.

She removed the muffins from the oven. The scent of the always popular strawberry cream cheese delights infused the room. Orange marmalades were already in the showcase, along with chocolate chip sour cream muffins that were the new rave these days.

She hurried because she still had to make the lemon muffins and more. She was thankful Tate had arrived when he did or these chocolate muffins would have burned and that would have smelled the bakery up for the morning. Thankfully, Trena should be arriving soon and that would help her catch up.

She needed to mix up several more batches of different flavors because lately the clientele had been growing and the muffins were getting more and more popular, so she probably should have done more than she'd baked. Her brain was mentally calculating everything she had to do. Plus, worrying that Trena was going to be late, she mixed faster. Customers would be arriving any minute.

Tate walked out of the back room; she glanced at him, met his gaze, and her fickle pulse instantly skyrocketed.

He relaxed nonchalantly against the doorframe, crossed his arms, and studied her. "You keep frowning like that and your face is going to freeze. That's what my mom used to tell my sisters when they were frowning."

"Well, she might be right, but at the moment I don't care."

"Are you always this grumpy or is it just with me?"

"No. I'm sorry. I'm just going a little bit crazy here."

He moved then to come stand beside her, his face concerned. "What's wrong? What can I help with? You do look a little uptight and frustrated, but I just assumed it was your dislike of me. I do have that effect on you."

"Well, don't kid yourself—yes, you do have that effect on me. But I'm behind and I'm going to have people walking in that door within the next twenty minutes and I don't have all of the muffins mixed up yet. It means that I could run out. And I'm worried that Trena might show up late. I've just got a lot on my mind and Rosie is counting on me to run this bakery the right way. And the last two days have not been going as smoothly as I anticipated."

"Well then, here, tell me what to do. I'm a pretty quick learner."

She stared at him. "You're serious?"

"Very. Anyway, I might not want to eat those amazing-smelling muffins but it might be kind of fun learning how to make them. You know...could be a secret weapon or something."

"Okay, go wash your hands and let's get to it... Is the freezer fixed?"

"Yeah, it was just a fuse. All I had to do was reset it and it's back to working."

"Give me a break—that's all it was?"

"Yeah and actually, it is a break for you. You don't have a bad freezer. You're off the hook. Now let me wash my hands and you show me what I need to do."

She watched him as he limped to the sink and turned the water on. *Holy moly, what had she just gotten herself into?*

CHAPTER SEVEN

What had he gotten himself into?

Tate washed his hands at the sink as his brain registered that he had just volunteered to make muffins. He was a stuntman: he fell out of planes, dove off cliffs, rode runaway cars down mountainsides—he did not make muffins. But one glance over his shoulder at the voluptuous brunette who was gathering supplies behind him and he knew that for as long as she wanted him today, he would be doing exactly that.

After he got his hands washed, he texted his mom and asked her whether she would drop by to pick up the muffins and take them to Rosie. He was pretty sure that Rosie had concocted this idea of bringing her muffins just to get him to come by and be around Gigi. But just in case she really wanted muffins for breakfast and a cup of her Bake My Day special blend coffee, he knew his mother would be overjoyed to be able to do something to help her very special daughter-in-law who was giving her her very first grandchild. The grandchild that Maryetta Sinclair had pretty much been going a little bit crazy over wishing for. Only after he had texted her did he realize that her coming to the shop and finding out that he was helping Gigi bake muffins was not going to go unnoticed. She would be over-the-moon excited; she would probably be rubbing her hands together in glee, thinking that she had another daughter-in-law on the horizon. He needed to keep this low-key.

Yeah, right. There was no way this was going to be low-key. Everyone would know and as soon as Mami, or Lila, or Doreen, or Birdie came by—or all of them at the same time because they did like to have coffee here—he was toast. But as he turned away from his phone, walked over to stand beside Gigi, and she lifted those beautiful eyes to his—he didn't care what anybody thought. He was going to enjoy himself.

And who knew—stuntmen needed to eat muffins too. Better yet, they needed to make muffins. He could be anywhere around the world, stuck in a rented apartment for an extended period of time, and he would know how to make muffins.

The idea that he would be somewhere around the world in an apartment that was rented while life went on in this hometown community that he enjoyed spending time in whenever he did get home suddenly didn't feel quite as exciting as it usually did to him. It seemed lonely.

"Okay, stuntman, let's get you to baking. Grab that measuring cup over there and dip it into that big bag of flour right there. Get me that whole big container full."

"That big container right there?"

"Yup—we're fixing to make a lot of muffins."

He eyed the big cup that had to be ten cups. What did he know? Last time he used a measuring cup was probably when he took his mom up on a bet when he was a teenager and made some brownies. That did not turn out so well. "Hopefully this is going to turn out better than my brownie experience back in high school." He hadn't thought about that in years.

She looked at him with interest. "You make brownies?"

"Oh no, that's the whole deal. My mom challenged me to make some brownies and cocky me thought, *Oh, what's the big deal?* I burned the brownies. They were horrible and I practically started a house fire. We got it out but it was an experience. And nobody in my family ever let me live it down. Although, lately, they seemed to have forgotten it so I'm hoping when they all find out we've been making muffins that we don't start rumors up again. But that's only if we don't burn the place down. If we burn Bake My Day down because of me trying to make muffins, you know I'll never get over that."

"If we burn Bake My Day down, the town would never get over that and, yes, your name would be mud."

He looked at her. "Well then, you better stay close to me and make sure I don't mess up." He meant those words far more than he had meant anything in a long time. The idea of having her close was very appealing to him. Maybe this would be a way to get past this somewhat cold shoulder she had to him because she was determined that them dating was not a good idea. Her past was holding her back from living life to the fullest. He believed in living life like a challenge and maybe that was why her backing away from living her life to the fullest bothered him so much.

As he dipped the measuring cup into the tub of flour, he glanced at her; she had flour on her cheek and on her forehead. He liked it. She gave of herself—full out—to help others; she was all in on that score. But not for herself.

He left the measuring cup in the flour and she looked up at him.

"You need that flour," she said.

He smiled. "I know." He paused, nodding toward her. "You have flour on your cheek." He lifted his hand and touched her cheek. Her gaze froze on his.

Her skin was soft and warm. His heart hammered and a longing so fierce to lean in and kiss her lips nearly ambushed him into doing exactly that. "There…all gone." His voice sounded as though he'd just eaten gravel.

He pulled his attention back to the flour. "Now what?" he asked as he dipped the large measuring cup.

He did as he was told but knew he was more than interested in this beautiful woman.

* * *

Working beside Tate was driving her crazy. Crazy was the only way to describe the way that her system bombarded her with bells and whistles and sirens. Every little thing she did set something off in her that warned her to stay back—stay away from him. A good thing, too, considering she kept finding herself leaning in toward him as she showed him how to hold the spatula just right while he scraped the edges of the large mixing bowl. Not only that, she kept accidentally touching his hands as she handed him ingredients. It was *crazy*.

She didn't want to get mixed up with a guy who had wanderlust in his blood and threw himself at risky adventure. She was risk-adverse and a homebody, for crying out loud, and yet here she was, making orange marmalade muffins and strawberry cream cheese delights with the man. The man who delighted everything in her whenever his eyes met hers, or his shoulder brushed hers, or his fingertips brushed hers.

She knew that when the bakery opened and patrons started coming in, certain patrons would be able to take one look at her, hot and flustered, and see right through any denial she might attempt. And that included not only Doreen, Birdie, Lila, and Mami but also Tate's mother. Yes, he had texted his mother to come by and get Rosie's muffins and coffee. The excited woman arrived almost instantaneously after he sent the text.

And she walked in when Gigi was flustered. Who wouldn't get flustered after he had gently brushed flour from her cheek and looked so deeply into her eyes that she thought for a moment he was going to kiss her and she was going to let him? Both of them found sanity in the midst of madness and started mixing muffins. But that didn't halt the turmoil and tingles raging through her—and, of course, probably pink, flushed cheeks.

"I came the moment I got your text," Maryetta declared as she strode to the counter and beamed at them across the top of it. Her expectant gaze darted from Tate to Gigi like a kid in a toy store. "I'm so thrilled that you're helping poor Gigi out in our Rosie's time of need," she said, almost breathless, as if she had run the distance from her home to the bakery. But of course she'd driven because their home was on the other side of town. "And thank you for calling me. I will be so excited to help that sweet, darling girl out any way that I can. We need the best for my grandbaby."

"Hey, Mom. Thanks for taking up the slack for me. We'll get you the order in just a second. I have to scrape the sides of this bowl like my instructor here has been telling me to do. Scraping bowls in these big mixers is obviously a very needed and demanding job. I'm getting pretty good at it. I can't say I'm getting any better at anything else but I can scrape some bowls with the best of them."

"Oh, dear, you aren't letting him near the oven, I hope. Has he told you how he almost burned the house down, attempting to bake brownies?" Maryetta's eyes widened in exaggerated alarm.

Gigi chuckled; she couldn't help it. "He did tell me that. Rest assured, Mrs. Sinclair, he is definitely a good bowl scraper, but I will monitor him at all times. We do not plan on burning down Rosie's bakery while she is out with your first grandchild."

"Wonderful. You sound like you have him all under control."

Tate gave his mother a playful glare. "I will not be controlled."

His mom smiled at him, then winked at Gigi. "Ignore him. I like what I'm seeing."

Gigi grinned at him. "Me too." She did not mean it that way but Tate hiked a sexy brow and sent her insides swirling. *Whew, he was gorgeous.* "By the time I'm finished with him, he'll be very qualified. As take-charge as he is, he will probably just come in your kitchen and take over."

"I wouldn't go that far," he cut in.

Maryetta looked as if she were on cloud nine. Gigi wanted to groan. *How was she ever going to convince everyone that there was nothing between her and Tate?* And that there never could be or would be. Especially when her own traitorous hormones were screaming for her to let go, be happy and live in the moment. To embrace this hunk of baking man goodness and never look back.

Not happening.

The man was more than likely leaving. She knew what risk was and she couldn't do it. Period. No matter how tempting Tate Sinclair, stuntman extraordinaire, was to her.

"I'll get the muffins for you. I think that today we'll send Rosie these fresh and always delectable blueberry muffins with the buttery cream insides. The woman is a genius when it comes to creating muffins and this is one of my favorites. So that's what she'll get today. And I'll get her a nice tall cup of coffee. While I'm doing that, can I get you some, too,

Maryetta? I know how you like your coffee."

"Thank you. I would love that. And you might throw me in one of those muffins also. I like the blueberry. And may I say that you two look absolutely stunning back there together. Tate, you should think about helping out here more often. Thank you for teaching him a few things. All men need to know their way around a kitchen—helps them impress a future wife. And muffins would be an extra plus."

Tate paused in his work. Gigi suspected that he was paying extreme attention on what he was doing to avoid a conversation like this with his mother. But Gigi knew enough about Maryetta to know that avoidance was not something you could do when she was around; she would pinpoint what she wanted and go for it.

"Don't you think that's an attractive attribute for a man, Gigi?"

"Mom," Tate said.

"Don't you Mom me." Her eyes twinkled as she smiled at Gigi. "Well, don't you?"

Being backed in a corner was not a place Gigi

wanted to be. "Um, I think I'll get Rosie's coffee ready." She spun and headed straight over to the coffee machine and began making Rosie's large decaffeinated Americano with a splash of caramel and monk fruit for sweetener. She busied herself with the machines and getting the Americano brewed exactly right. Once she did that, she brewed a second cup for Maryetta.

Tate was telling his mother all about their morning escapade with the freezer and how it ended up just being a blown fuse. Maryetta asked several questions and Tate answered, all the while giving Gigi time to get the coffee done.

Gigi boxed up the muffins and handed over the coffee and was relieved a few minutes later. "Here you go. Please tell Rosie we've got it covered."

Maryetta took the coffee carrier and the bag. "Oh, I certainly will. You two have fun today." She smiled widely, waved good-bye, and headed out of the store.

Gigi took a deep breath, then looked over at Tate. "Whew. That was intense."

"Don't let her get to you." His expression was amused. "She's getting a bit obnoxious these days."

She laughed. "Is that what you call that?"

"Yeah, so I apologize now for anything my mother might do in the coming days or weeks. I'd like to hope she gives me my space but I have no idea how badly she'll cross the line, getting into my business."

He was telling the truth, and she understood it. Rosie had talked about how hard her mother-in-law was pushing to have all of her kids married and pregnant.

"Maybe she'll back off. But right now, we need to put that batter in muffin pans before the door swings open and we get a herd of customers in. I hope you're ready to rock and roll."

He laughed. "I'm ready to see how these muffins turn out."

She wanted to tell him she could handle it for the rest of the day but instead, she stepped back beside him, breathing in the scent of him rather than the muffin batter, and knew as long as he wanted to help, she would let him.

CHAPTER EIGHT

The week had been interesting. Three days of Tate helping her in the bakery, had been nerve-racking. The man was amazing. He had filled orders, smiled at customers and laughed at himself when he messed up—and the customers had laughed with him. When he was putting three muffins in a bag and dropped the bag, causing the muffins to roll out onto the floor, he had instantly taken charge by picking them up, tossing them into the air and starting to juggle them.

Unbelievable. As she watched him juggle the three

blueberry muffins with the precision of a well-seasoned juggler, making the crowd of women squeal with delight, she knew he was going to be a tough act to follow. She couldn't juggle and even if she could she wouldn't look like he did while doing it. The man was one lean mean working machine and she never knew juggling muffins would show off so many muscles! His pecks were flexing and his biceps were bulging and even his already rock hard abs appeared to tighten beneath his form-fitting T-shirt as he moved slightly to stay centered with the moving muffins.

"I could watch you do that all day," Mami said, and leveled her mischievous gaze on her. "Couldn't you, Gigi?"

All eyes tore themselves off of Tate momentarily to land on her. Oh, boy. "Well, I might not date much but I'm not dead." What else could she say? Her words brought lots of agreements.

"That's good to hear," Tate said, winking at her as he glanced at her and immediately dropped a muffin to the floor. She bit back a laugh.

"Look what you did to me. Got me all shook up,"

he laughed, as they both bent to pick up the muffins.

They both grabbed for the same one and he ended up holding her hand as she clutched the muffin. She looked into his smiling eyes and her insides warmed.

"I'll get this," he said, turning her hand over as she just stared breathlessly at him.

What was wrong with her? "I've got this one." She yanked her hand away and jumped to her feet to find Mami, Birdie, Lila and Doreen watching them with glee in their eyes. The other customers were too, but thankfully as far as she knew they were not here with matchmaking on their minds.

"Okay, shows over. Who's up next," she called, as she tossed the muffin in the garbage can as if it was a basketball.

"Two points," Tate said as the muffin dropped into the trash can without hitting any rims. He followed her lead and shot the other two muffins into the can with perfect precision too.

"Four points for you. Now let's try for that to be the last of Rosie's muffins that go in the trash."

"I agree. No more juggling or dropping pretty pink

bags full of muffins." Tate raised his hand as if taking a solemn oath.

"But it was so entertaining," Lila said, looking crestfallen. "Maybe you could juggle tennis balls instead. I loved watching you."

"You are very talented," Doreen said. "I tried to juggle but large boobs and short arms do not a juggler make."

The room erupted with laughter and Tate actually blushed. Poor Doreen was not hardly five feet tall, and very top heavy, her statement was completely true.

"Wow, you're actually turning pink," she whispered to him as she walked to the coffee machine to start the coffee orders she knew the regulars were about to order after the laughter died down.

"Yeah, you didn't warn me about this part of the job," he said, leaning close as she passed by.

She laughed softly. "Okay, let's get to work. You fill the muffins and I'll fill the coffee orders."

He winked at her and then turned back to the counter. "Okay, ladies you heard the lady, let's get down to business. Hit me with your orders and let the coffee and muffin joy begin.

* * *

Tate was waiting beside Gigi's Mustang at closing time. He had left after Trena had arrived for work after the lunch hour. It was five o'clock now and he had Gigi on his mind.

She paused as soon as she locked the door of the bakery and spotted him leaning against her car.

His pulse was pumping like a jackhammer as she started walking again, her gaze locked on his. "Hey, thought I'd come by and get my raincheck."

She stopped a foot in front of him. "Raincheck?"

"Yeah, the night I rescued you, you said you'd give me a ride in this amazing car of yours."

"I did say that, didn't I?"

"Yes, how about a drive along the coast?"

She bit her lip and he could practically see her mind rolling over options. To his surprise she held out her keys. "You can drive with that boot on your left foot, right?"

He grinned and took the keys. "I can drive. Hop in, top down?"

She laughed, and walked to the passenger side of the car. "Is there any other way on a gorgeous day like today?"

"I knew you were a woman after my own heart the night I carried you out and saw this car."

She climbed into the passenger seat and he behind the wheel. He cranked the engine and it purred to life with the rumble of a powerful motor beneath the hood. "This is going to be fun."

She smiled, leaned over and pushed a button and the top lowered. "That was a modification I love about the car."

"Me too."

She leaned her head back and relaxed rolling her head toward him. "I'm going to enjoy this."

Tate liked seeing her relaxed like this. "Good, that makes two of us. And the best part is it's just the two of us with no nosy little ladies watching our every move."

"You are so right," she laughed and he did too.

He pulled out onto the road and drove.

* * *

By the time Gigi closed the doors of Bake My Day early on Tuesday afternoon four days after her ride in her Mustang with Tate, a tropical storm had been brewing off the coast for a couple of days. Almost mirroring the storm that had been brewing inside her since that ride and having worked beside him those few days. She let the wind wash over her as she stared down the street toward the blue water visible from the bakery's location. The wind had picked up considerably as reports had come in saying that the tropical storm would reach them by midnight. It wasn't expected to be horrible but it would batter them a good bit. Gigi was used to storms but right now her insides were storming just as badly as any storm that was on its way.

She strode to her car, glancing around the vacant parking area. The town had cleared out some; people were home preparing for the storm. She pulled her phone out of her pocket as she slid in behind the steering wheel and glanced once again at the weather report, she'd weathered worse. It wasn't a hurricane— it was clearly just a tropical storm.

She cranked her car and pulled away from the bakery, headed toward her bungalow. As she drove past the bed-and-breakfast owned by Erin Sinclair— soon to be Nash Bond's wife—she saw Erin and Nash moving a potted plant off her front porch. Erin saw her and a huge smile flashed across her face as she waved.

Gigi waved as she drove by. No doubt Erin had heard that her brother Tate had helped her out at the bakery. Tate helping her in the bakery had added fuel to the fire about them and someone had seen them driving out of town in her car and that too had stoked the gossip grapevine. After seeing Tate in a kitchen, baking business had been busier because he was a sight to see. Tate was already the heartthrob of the town so people were naturally drawn to him even other places. The man with the mostess. The phrase rang through her head. "Who is driving me crazy," she muttered.

She kept having to remind herself that he would

leave soon.

She just had to survive until he left. She had to have a plan; she had to get a plan together and stick to it and protect herself.

A strong gust of wind slammed against her small car and she had to hold the wheel with both hands to keep it from crossing over the yellow line. *Goodness, that wind was picking up.* As she pulled into the subdivision that she lived in, she noticed that it was also vacant. They hadn't had too much bad weather this fall and she suspected that people were overreacting because it was basically the first time this year and they didn't want to get caught unprepared.

She pushed the button and her little tiny garage door lifted. She drove into the single-car bay, pushed the button, and watched the garage door lower behind her. She got out of the car and unlocked the door leading into the kitchen. She dropped her keys into the little brown wooden bowl she kept there on her counter so she could always find them and then she headed toward her bedroom.

She stripped off her shirt and her jeans and her

undergarments, and stepped into a warm shower. She needed to wash the muffin scent off her. She didn't always do that but some days the sweetness of where she worked just coated her and when she came home, she liked to get it off immediately. Today, she needed the hot shower not only to gt the scent of the muffins off her but just to basically give her a wake-up call. She ducked her head under the hot spray and let the droplets run onto her skin and hoped that when she got out, she was thinking a little more clearly.

Minutes later as she dried off with a towel and stared at her reflection in the mirror, she knew she wasn't thinking any more clearly than she had been earlier. At least she didn't smell like sweet muffins, but she was sure thinking about one sweet, helpful, gorgeous man... Tate Sinclair was unforgettable. And she needed to forget him.

She dressed in her comfy sweats and padded barefoot into the kitchen, where she turned on the TV. She grabbed the remote, flipped it to the Weather Channel, and got the news on what was coming toward her beloved little town. You never knew when to believe the news—they exaggerated so badly sometimes. Just last year, they said that this hurricane was coming directly toward them and everyone overreacted, but it went two thousand miles or wherever up the coast of Texas. It cost their little town so much in tourist revenue because everybody was fearful that the hurricane was coming and they canceled reservations. Sunset Bay had barely gotten any wind from that hurricane and many of the businesses had suffered that fall.

Hopefully tonight they wouldn't go crazy with their reporting. According to them, the storm was bearing down on them and wouldn't be life-threatening. So at least they were not going crazy. She was certain that they had been made aware of the economic trouble they had caused and maybe—just maybe—they were being more cautious. At least she hoped so.

She opened the refrigerator and pulled out some leftover chicken that she'd had the night before. She began to slice the chicken up to make a chicken salad. She had everything she needed, and a good chicken salad sandwich on a croissant that she had picked up yesterday would be lovely. She tried hard not to let her thoughts go back to the time over the last week working with Tate. She'd hoped it would only be for a day but then Kelly had called in and her car had completely broken down; plus she was sick so she had been out the whole week and Trena had already planned to be out of town. Obviously she had needed help and Tate had offered to step in. He'd helped out for five days. *Five days!*

Trena had returned today, thank goodness. Because Gigi hadn't been sure she could survive another day beside Tate without doing something she would really and truly regret.

* * *

Tate woke during the night, rolled over in his bed, and stared out the open window. He realized that the storm that had been brewing off the coast had come inland. The wind bashed at the window and rain pelted it. He got out of bed, raked a hand through his tussled hair, and strode closer to the window. Lightning struck somewhere on the horizon and he saw how ferocious the waves were as the night sky lit up. Realization hit that this was going to be worse than anyone had expected.

He turned and limped over to grab his phone off the side table. He glanced at the weather report—they were under a warning. He headed to the kitchen, his mind going to Gigi. *Was she prepared for the storm?*

She had lived here for a long time and she knew the precautions to takc, knew that tropical storms could shift and change direction quickly. He knew his own family was very well prepared as always, but his family had each other. It had become very apparent to him just in the short time he had become reacquainted with Gigi that, though she worked at the bakery around people all the time, she really kept to herself.

Was she as alone as he thought she was?

He stood at the counter, staring out at the windows, and realized that he needed to close the shutters. Hurrying to his room, the boot on his leg making him want to yank it off and sling it across the room, he grabbed his hip-length slicker from his closet and shoved his arms into it as he moved toward the sliding glass door. He slid it open and let himself out onto the very wet deck. If he hadn't had the slicker on, he would have been soaked in seconds. His athletic shorts and his legs were soaked. His bare foot and the boot were also.

He'd been through worse and ignored it all as he grabbed the metal shutters, unlocked them, and then pulled them across the door to protect the glass. He pulled the smaller shutters across the windows, locked them all down, and then carefully moved to the side of the house, where he let himself inside through the side entrance door. He stood on the mat, letting the water drip onto it as he slipped the soaked rain jacket off.

He then strode to the bedroom bath, grabbed towels and dried off. He sat on the side of the bed and unstrapped the Velcro straps holding the boot on. He pulled the contraption off, flexing his ankle, glad to feel it stronger and with almost no pain. He threw the towels on the floor, stood and then eased back to the dresser, grabbed clothes and yanked them on. Testing his bad ankle, he moved into the kitchen, where he grabbed the mop and strode back to his room. He mopped the water from the floor in the bathroom, bedroom, and followed his trail through the house. Once that was done, he grabbed his rubber boots and a dry pair of socks. Once he had on his dry jeans and T-shirt, he pulled the dry socks on and then stuck one jean-clad leg into one of his rubber boots, the other one back into the wet orthopedic boot that he ran a towel over to dry out as much as possible.

He heard the loud boom of thunder as he moved back into the living room. He checked the weather report again and though it wasn't a hurricane, the storm was really close to becoming one. The winds were crazy. Unable to help himself, he grabbed his keys and his slicker, and went out to the small garage that housed his truck. He threw everything into the backseat, grabbed an emergency light off the workbench, and climbed inside his vehicle. He pushed the button and watched his garage door open.

The storm had the palm trees near his drive going crazy. He backed out, pushed the button and as he turned back onto the street, the garage door closed. He glanced at his yard and saw things that had been sitting upright turned over. A plant in a heavy glass container had been knocked off the front porch and deck chairs that had been on the front porch had been flipped over and thrown in the yard. He put the truck in drive and headed down his road at a fast clip. Yeah, he was acting territorial but he needed to check on Gigi. He drove through town; seeing things torn up and water rising, his concern grew. His rental was built up on higher ground; access to the beach was a walk down stairs from his deck. Flooding wasn't a problem.

But Gigi had a view from her yard and she wasn't on higher ground. Flooding would be a big problem for her, he feared.

The rain slapped against the windshield and the wipers were working overtime to make it to where he had a vague view through the glass. The closer he drove toward Gigi's, the more he knew for those in the lower areas flooding was likely. Gigi's bungalow especially.

What would she think when he showed up? She

was as attracted to him as he was to her but she was fighting it. Very hard. And he got it, after what she'd told him about her ex. He'd struggled all week since they'd made muffins together not to push her too hard. But he knew with deep certainty he wanted to get to know her better. He had gotten to work with her several days and enjoyed every moment of it. And their car ride down the coast had been nice. He'd been tempted to try and get closer to her that day but had just enjoyed the ride and her company. Now Trena had come back to work and he was back to seeing Gigi when he went by to pick up Rosie's muffins. This morning he'd lingered and talked some, enjoying every moment. He thought she had too, but she'd been pulling back also he felt. Like she knew she was letting her guard down with him and she didn't want to.

He decided he probably wouldn't even knock on her door if everything looked fine. But if it didn't look fine, he would knock on her door and offer to help her. As he drove into her neighborhood, he saw that the homes that were at the beginning of the road seemed to be fine. But the water was running down the street, downhill, toward her home at the end of the cul-de-sac.

All his plans changed when his headlights landed on her home and he spotted her in the beam of his lights, a yellow slicker moving quickly in the yard as lightning flashed overhead.

Gigi was carrying sandbags.

He parked his truck then scrambled out as fast as his booted ankle would let him. He pulled his own slicker back on as he stormed across the yard to help. The wind whipped and pushed as he headed toward her. He ignored it.

"What are you doing here?" she called over the wind. Her dark hair was plastered to her head; strands were stuck to her cheek and she looked tired. But beautiful and determined.

"I'm here to help. I woke up to the storm and I knew that you were probably in danger of flooding. I thought that you might need a helping hand. Is the water rising in back too?"

Rain pelted her face. She was soaked despite the rain jacket. "Yes. If I don't get the sandbags in place, it won't be long until I have water inside. I wasn't expecting it but thankfully I keep them ready. Still, it caught me off guard. The water's already to the patio."

"Show me where to get some and I'll help."

She pointed toward her garage and he headed that way as she carried the large bag she held around the side of the house.

He grabbed two, heaving one to each shoulder, and then hurried after her. He found her bent over, placing the sandbag on top of the small area that she was trying to do around the door that would help divert the water away from her back door. He quickly laid what he had on top of hers. Wind came and battered her; she stumbled and would have fallen if he hadn't grabbed her arm and pulled her close. She was pressed against him and, looking down into her wide eyes, he was so tempted in that moment to bend down and kiss her.

"Do you do this often?" he asked, trying to lighten the mood and so very glad that he'd come.

"More than I really want to. But I've managed to only have major damage once and preventative measures are my only saving grace."

He wanted to tell her that now he could be part of that. He was amazed how quickly he'd become engaged with her on a more personal level. Quicker than she probably wanted, but he was there. And he wasn't exactly sure what to do about it, except right now she needed his help and she was going to get it. The kiss could wait until later.

CHAPTER NINE

Gigi couldn't believe that Tate had come to help her. She hadn't expected anybody to be here to help her. She never asked for help and always managed on her own. Although, when there was a huge storm coming and she needed help, she knew she could call on all of her friends. One call and she would have had help. But old habits were hard to break. When she and her mother had needed help, they'd struggled and not asked for it and they'd managed. Barely, but they had survived. Until her mother had died.

"Gigi, are you okay?"

Tate's concerned voice brought her back from her unhappy memories. "I'm fine." She stared up at him. He hadn't asked; he had just shown up. It was after midnight and he had been woken by the storm and thought of her. The very thought sent a shiver of warmth flowing through her. She pushed from his arms. "I better get busy."

She hurried away from him, toward the front of the house. Her heart thundered as she grabbed another sandbag. She could only carry one at a time but he could carry two, even with the rehab boot on his foot. He walked awkwardly past her to retrieve another bag. They were working against time but he just kept right on going, that slick boot on the mud and the water. Every time she looked at him as they passed each other, he would wink at her, or smile at her or let her know that it was okay. They were going to make it. Just his look of encouragement was enough to lift her spirits. Because the thought of the house flooding hadn't been a good one for her. In the last tropical storm, she had some water damage, and hadn't wanted a repeat.

When the last sandbag was in place and the water was being held back, he put his hands on his hips and gave her a reassuring smile. "I don't know how long this is going to hold, but let's go inside and maybe you can get dried off a little bit and then we'll wait it out. If it doesn't slack up and starts looking like it's coming in the door, we can get your furniture up off the ground, stacking it on top of each other so at least some of it won't get ruined. I can call my brothers out, too, and they can bring more sandbags if we need them to."

"Okay," she said. Her adrenaline was slowing and her legs felt like jelly. As she started to step over the sandbag, she tripped, but once again he reached for her. Only this time he swept her into his arms, holding her against his hard chest. Her hands were on his chest and she looked into his dark eyes. The wind howled around them and she clung to him. Suddenly, all she wanted was to kiss him. To thank him for having come to her rescue.

Again.

The man had been coming to her rescue almost daily since he'd arrived in town.

His jaw tightened as she placed a hand gently against his jaw. "We're going to have to stop meeting like this," she said, her voice barely audible above the wind.

"I'll take you in my arms any way I can get you," he said, his voice husky. "You okay?"

"Yes." His words had her breath catching and her pulse raging like the storm. She nodded, not trusting her voice. He tilted his head toward her, their lips so close. *He was going to kiss her.*

He paused. "Come on. We better get you out of this rain. I-I don't know what I was thinking."

She knew what she wished he was thinking. The thought was so not what she wanted to be thinking but it was exactly what she was thinking and wanting. *A kiss from her hero.*

But it was totally against everything that she knew was right.

She didn't want him to kiss her; she didn't want him to want her or anything like that. The man was leaving and that was all she needed to know. And yet, right now, right here, in his arms, she didn't want to think about that. All she wanted was for him to wrap those strong, hard-muscled arms around her tighter and to hold her closer.

He was her shelter against the storm and she wondered what it would be like to have him beside her against all the storms that life might bring her way.

What was she thinking? "Please, put me down. I can walk now. I promise not to stumble again."

He did as she asked, as if he needed distance as much as she did. She moved out of his arms, stepped over the sandbag as he kept his hand firmly on her elbow and then he followed her into the house after she slid the door open. They both stepped into the tiled kitchen/living room space of her small bungalow and he closed the door behind them. Instantly, the sound quieted and it felt good to be out of the wind.

"Wait here and I'll grab some towels." She slid out of her slicker and let it drop to the tiled floor, then she hurried into the utility room. A stack of folded towels sat on the dryer; she grabbed an armload then headed back to where Tate waited.

He had removed his slicker and stood there in jeans, and a very wet T-shirt that outlined every muscular inch of his torso. The slicker must have leaked in around the neckline because it hadn't protected him very much. The man was in amazing shape and why not? He was a stuntman, after all—they had to be in ultimate shape. She told herself to get a grip.

"Here you go." She held out two towels to him and he took them.

"Thanks."

She busied herself drying off her face, arms, and neck. Then she held the towel to her as it dried some of the water off her legs that had been exposed beneath her slicker. "I'll see if I can find something for you, although I don't have any men's clothing…wait, I may have a pair of warmups or an oversized pair of mine."

"That might work, although if they belong to you, they better be really oversized."

She chuckled. "You can wear them pushed up around your knees."

"Cute, I'm sure."

She chuckled as she headed to her room, closing the door behind her. She tugged off her wet pajama bottoms and grabbed a pair of jeans, tugged them on her cold legs then pulled on a fresh shirt. She then dug through her closet and came up with an oversized pair of sweats that had belonged to Bill. She had forgotten about Bill leaving those at her house, recalling that he'd lent them to her to wear home after her pants had gotten paint on them one day when she'd been helping him paint his living room. A living room she'd thought would be shared by her when they got married. She'd been making plans for their future and he'd been making plans to leave. She stared at them. Sour memories gurgled in her stomach and she wanted to throw them out the door and get rid of them now that she knew they were here in her house. But she was an adult and Tate could use them now.

"These will have to do," she said to herself and then strode back into the kitchen.

Tate was at the coffeemaker, his back to her, the toned muscles of his back setting the sourness of her stomach aside.

"Hope you don't mind—I thought I might make some coffee."

She held out the sweatpants to him. "That sounds great. I found these. I had forgotten that I had them."

He took them, staring at them. "These aren't yours?"

"No. Kind of a flash from the past. But they'll work for you."

He hitched a brow then started walking and stopped. "Where can I change into these not-so-good-flash-from-the-past warmups?"

She smiled at him, unable to help herself. "You can go in my room. There's a bathroom in there too."

He nodded and then disappeared into her room. *He was in her room. Why had she sent him into her room?* Because this house didn't have a second bedroom. It was a one-bedroom bungalow that she had just been lucky enough to get when she moved back here. She hadn't needed anything bigger.

By the time he emerged from the bedroom, carrying his wet jeans, she had poured them both a cup of coffee. He went into the utility room and tossed his jeans into the dryer. She heard the door open, heard it close and then him crank the loud dryer knob, and then he was back. She held the coffee out to him. He took it from her; his hand brushed hers and sent heated flames of unwanted attraction shooting through her.

Tate held his arms out and twisted his hips. "Your unwanted flash from the past fits me pretty good. Obviously, whoever these belonged to was about my size."

"Yes." Gigi frowned. Her gaze drifted down him then sprang back to his face. Heat burned her cheeks. "Thanks for coming. I still can't believe you came," she said, changing the subject. "I can't believe you just woke up and then thought of me."

Why had she said that?

He leaned against the kitchen counter and studied her over his coffee cup. He looked so handsome, with his wet hair and jawline with a subtle stubble to it and those penetrating blue eyes that seemed to dig into every shadowy section of her soul.

It was scary to her. *He would leave.*

The silence of the moment stretched between them and Gigi's heart pounded as she held Tate's probing gaze. The attraction and pull between them filled the space, as if she had no reason at all to not want to see where they—as in the two of them, as in this thing between them—could go from here. She bit her lip— not the right thing to do because it made her think about his lips and the fact that she wouldn't mind feeling them on hers. Not something she needed to be thinking about right now. Her house was about to flood; there was a storm raging outside and she was thinking about kissing the devastatingly, amazingly handsome man standing a mere twenty-four inches away from her. When his gaze dropped to her lips and then raised slowly back to her eyes, she had no doubt in her mind that he was thinking almost the exact same thing she was. *Oh boy.*

"Will the place you're staying at flood?" It was a question meant to change the sub-text floating between them.

But it was clearly just a question to fill the space. The way that his lip quirked at the edges told her he understood exactly why she had asked the question. Avoidance was something she had learned through the years. Avoiding personal questions or wants that had to do with herself, her past or her future, had become the norm for her.

"It's locked up and protected. It would take a Category 3 to 5 to knock that old place off its stilts. It's been around a long time."

She nodded, not sure what to say after that. She searched her brain and set her coffee cup down. He set his coffee cup down and stepped twelve inches closer, sliding along the edge of the countertop as if trying not to spook her. Her breathing increased and she tried to not heave in breaths to stop the shallow breathing. His gaze never left hers. And she could not look away.

"Do you know that I cannot stop thinking about you?" he asked, his voice low and so sexy.

It set off alarm bells that she needed to turn and run but she couldn't.

"Really?" She breathed the word. She couldn't stop thinking about him either. It was maddening really, and so dangerous to her. She knew that other people got happy endings but she didn't. Everyone important in her life had left her. She knew this; she knew it with every ounce of her soul. Her dad, her mother, Bill—and Tate would, too. And yet her brain couldn't compute the data that it was receiving. Instead, her mind had malfunctioned and was telling her to grab him and hang on. She had completely lost her mind. "I shouldn't think of you but I do."

As if that were all the words he needed, he slid his arm behind her on the counter, wrapped his finger around her hip, and gently tugged her to him. He was as strong and muscular and hard as she had believed. As she had remembered. But now, as both of his arms wrapped around her and his gaze stayed locked with hers, she lost all thought.

"I've been wanting to kiss you from the first moment I saw you at the wedding that night with those big eyes and that pretty mouth of yours shaped in that cute *O*, as if you had just gasped over what that crazy door had done to your dress."

"That's exactly what I was doing."

"And then you spoke and were so sassy. I've been

hooked ever since."

She had been thinking the same thoughts about him ever since she had turned and found him there. But she had been in complete denial.

"I think it's time." He breathed the words and then he lowered his head to hers. And then slowly, tenderly, his lips moved over hers and she was completely and utterly lost.

* * *

The kiss was like nothing he had ever experienced. Tate had kissed many women, he couldn't deny it, but never with his whole being. There was more involved in this kiss than just physical attraction and tantalizing sparks. This went deeper and it stunned him as her arms slid around his neck and she responded to his kiss. He deepened the kiss, pulling her closer.

It felt oh so right to him. But he knew that Gigi was tender; she had already told him she didn't want to have a relationship with him. Her words and her actions right now weren't going together well. *What would she think?*

And his gut told him to get hold of himself. He pulled back. She opened her eyes; they were dazed and so beautiful. *He could get lost in those eyes for the rest of his life.* The thought startled him. "I think I better go, or—" he said, just as a crash sounded outside and lightning lit the sky. The windows rattled. "Or maybe I just need to find out what that was."

He dropped his arms from around her and moved to the window. The water was rising and if the rain didn't stop soon, her home would flood. He turned to her. "We better start stacking your things. You tell me what's most important. We need to put what we can on your bed. Do you have blocks to put your bed up on or your tables?"

She sprang into action. "I do." She hurried into the bedroom and he followed her. She pulled out four large blocks of wood and placed them at the foot of the bed. He grabbed the footboard and lifted and she stuck two blocks under the bed. He moved to the head of the bed; first on one side, he lifted and she stuck a block under it and then moved to the other side and did the same.

"Okay, how about the dressers—do you want them on there?"

"They're not the most important thing. I bought them at a thrift store. But the books in the bookcases and the dining room table."

"Let's start stacking. Tell me what you cherish the most."

For the next thirty minutes, they worked to get as much as they could, moving things off the floor and onto boxes or blocks that she pulled from a storage closet.

"You were prepared," he said as he stacked another box of things on the bed.

"I try to be."

"I like that about you. As someone who has to be prepared myself, I can relate to that."

She paused placing books in a plastic storage bin. "When you do a stunt?"

"Yes, or rappel down a mountain, or jump off a suspension bridge. Believe me, it pays to prepare. Better prep means better adventure and that I live to have another adventure."

It was all true. She swallowed and looked alarmed. "I don't see how you can do that. It scares me for you. I bet your mother worries constantly."

"She lets me be me. We're all going to die someday. I want to live until I die." He winked but she was frozen, staring at him. "What?"

"You really aren't afraid?"

"People die every day—sitting in chairs, walking down steps, things we take for granted as harmless. When it's your time, it's your time, so I might as well do what I want to do."

"Yes, I understand that. I've lost plenty of people I loved…"

"Your mom and dad?"

"My mom and my grandparents."

"What about your dad?"

She looked sick for a second. "And my dad."

He wondered what had happened with her dad because her reaction wasn't normal. But he didn't ask. "I've lost my grandparents and some friends through the years but we're all going to lose loved ones. The key is loving them while we have them. And living…Life should be lived with no regrets."

She cleared her throat and blinked hard. "That's not always easy."

"Why do you say that? Suddenly she looked so sad and he had the urge to hug her. "I'd like to know," he urged, hoping she'd let him in.

"Some people don't value love." She sucked in a halting breath but instead of sharing more she nodded toward the door. "We better get busy. I see water."

He turned and saw water seeping in beneath the bottom of the door. It would flow faster if something weren't done fast. He looked out the window, water was flowing over the sandbags. "I'm going out the front door. I'll come around and restack them and then come back inside through the front door. We'll flood the place if we open this one. It will buy us some time."

CHAPTER TEN

Tate clunked out of the house with his blasted boot as fast as he could. He welcomed the rain on his face, clearing his fuddled brain. He had forgotten about the storm and everything as he'd kissed Gigi but then she'd pulled back and reminded him exactly how different they were. He loved his life, living it to its fullest—which did require some risk. She ran from risk.

They would never work as a couple, so what was he doing?

He made it around the edge of the house and then,

moving through the rushing water to the sandbags, he lifted the first one and placed it snug against the door. He restacked everything to where it was snug against the door. He saw Gigi watching him through the window. Her brow was etched with worry. He needed the rain to stop so the water would quit rising. He turned and moved back to the front of the house. The warmups were clinging to him and growing heavy from all the water. He was ready to get them off, not a fan of wearing her old boyfriend's pants. Hopefully his jeans were almost dry; if not, he'd be putting them on anyway.

When he made it to the door, she was there, waiting with more towels. "Thanks." He took one and scrubbed his hair and his face. "Maybe that bought us some time. I'll need my jeans now. Unless you have some more pants from the one you don't want to talk about somewhere."

She shook her head. "No more of those. I'll get your jeans."

She moved into the utility room as he stripped off his shirt and dried his arms and body as best he could.

When she returned, she paused at the door, seeing him without a shirt on. He guessed she looked at his chest and then moved forward to hand him the jeans and held a hand out for his shirt.

"I'll take that and put it in the dryer. You'll catch a cold standing there like that."

He laughed. "Yeah, I might."

He moved into the room and changed quickly into the blue jeans. They were still damp but not soaked. He took his phone after he changed and he called Brad.

"Hey, where are you?" he asked as soon as Brad answered.

"I'm at the firehouse. This storm has brought us all out. We're having to go in and make sure everyone's safe. Where are you?"

"I'm here at Gigi's house and she's getting in some water. Do you have any extra sandbags anywhere?"

"I do. Why are you at Gigi's? It's nearly three in the morning."

"I woke up at one and saw the storm. I knew she was alone and came to see if she needed help and she did. We've been working on getting the sandbags she had around the house, and get all of her stuff up on blocks but the water's starting to come in the door. We're safe. I can get out with my truck but I'm trying to keep her from taking on as much water as possible."

"I'll be over—give me a few minutes. See you then."

He hung up and looked at Gigi. "Brad's bringing more sandbags. Maybe they will hold off the water."

"Thank you. You've been such a help. And all the firemen—we really rely on them during times like this. Your brother really is an amazing fire chief. Everyone loves him."

He suddenly felt a little jealous of his brother. Tate was a stuntman; he basically risked his life for things that were, in the big realm of things, not really important. Brad was a fireman, a real hero. When Brad did a "stunt," it was real life, and his risk was not always calculated carefully on his side, like Tate's. "He's a good guy."

"Everyone here is grateful for him. And your brother Adam, too. We needed a new doctor when he came back."

Again, a stab of jealousy hit Tate. Brad and Adam had both dedicated their adventurous spirits to helping others. *Who did he help? His bank account.* Yes, he gave to charities but in the big picture of things, where did his true worth and value come in compared to his brothers and the choices they'd made? Even Jonah went out on rescues with his boats when needed. Recently he had saved a man whose boat sank in rough waters.

The thoughts of how he compared to his brothers suddenly gnawed at him. "I guess we better finish getting ready for him," he said, just as the lights went out.

* * *

Tate needed to get this boot off. He could feel all the water slogged down inside it and it was slipping, starting to become a dangerous mess. He sank to one of the chairs that had been beside the kitchen table and now sat pushed over against the wall. He unbuckled it.

Gigi walked over; he could feel her eyes on him as he concentrated on taking the boot off.

"Tate, let me take that. I'll put it up. Try to figure out something to help you get around with. That looks terrible…maybe I can clean the inside out."

"Thanks. Anything will help. I'll be so glad when I don't have to wear that anymore."

"Will you be able to get around right now or do I just need to dry it out and give it back to you?"

"I'll manage."

She took the boot from him and moved into the kitchen. He stood and leaned against the counter, testing his foot as she pulled a dish towel out and went to drying the boot. She had no more towels. They had stacked everything she had against the sliding glass door to try to hold off as much water as they could. For the moment, they were all being used to soak up the water coming under the door.

"The rain has stopped, and I see Brad's headlights." He moved, putting his weight on the ankle and realizing he could do it; he just needed to be careful.

"Stop! What do you think you're doing? You're not supposed to be walking on that."

"I'm fine. I need to help Brad."

She moved in front of the door, her hands on her hips. "Tate Sinclair, you are not going to injure your ankle worse helping me. You wait right there. I'll have this boot dried out some and then you can put it back on."

He took his hands and put them on her shoulders. He ignored the desire to wrap her in his arms. Instead, he moved her to the side. "I'm fine. Dry the boot out and I'll put it on when I come back in. I won't hurt my ankle. Adam has already told me it's almost time for it to come off anyway."

She wasn't happy, he could tell, but she moved away from him and went back to where she had been working on his boot. He opened the door and slipped outside. Brad was getting out of the back of the truck with sandbags in his arms. "Hey, thanks for coming."

Brad nodded at the truck. "There's more in the truck. Glad you called. I'd have been here sooner if I'd known. I'd have brought more help but everyone is out helping others. The rain looks like it's about over but we need to put these up just in case until it quits flowing."

"Exactly my thoughts. Thanks. Around back—you'll see it."

Brad had his rain gear on and he moved through the water; it was now mid-calf as he went into the lower area of the house, on the slope where all the water pooled. Walking in his socked feet, Tate moved slower, taking it easy on his ankle, not wanting to have to put that thing back on because he pushed too hard. Grabbing some more bags, he followed his brother, being careful as he walked. It didn't take them long. Brad was faster than he was to stack more sandbags in a thicker line to help hold off the water.

When they were done, they walked back to the truck. Both of them could have been wetter if the rain had been pounding but thankfully it had pretty much completely disappeared.

"Thanks. I think we might have saved her from too much damage."

Brad studied him. "My question to you is what

made you wake up in the middle of the night and think of Gigi? I've heard rumors. I saw you carrying her out of the wedding reception that night. I didn't know—"

"We haven't had a thing for each other, if that's what you're asking. Everyone seems to be thinking that but this just happened. I don't know. I haven't actually seen her but for some reason, that night, when she asked for my help, my eyes were opened and suddenly she's all I'm thinking about."

Brad grinned at him. "This is good. Mom will be thrilled that you're actually dating someone from home."

"She thinks something is going on but please don't say anything to her because there might not be anything to tell. Tonight, I came to help her but we are very different people. And though I would love to see more of her, she's been hurt and isn't real fond of my way of life. But she's doing something to my head and I'm thinking settling down might not be the craziest thing in the world."

"Seriously? Coming from you, I don't know if I believe that. Tate, you're not normal. I apologize if that sounds crazy…but you're not. You have this thing inside you that drives you to go. You haven't stuck around for any period of time in ten years. You come and go at a whim. So, you suddenly thinking about settling down—I don't know, I hate to be skeptical but I am."

Tate stepped back. "Yeah, I get why you would say that. Took me by surprise, too."

"Look," Brad looked almost apologetic, "Gigi is not the easiest person to get to know around town. She sticks to herself. She's very private with her problems but she's friendly and everybody likes her. Nobody would want to see her get hurt."

Tate raked a hand through his hair. "So what are you saying?"

"I'm saying be careful and think about her. Make sure you know what you want before you play with her heart."

* * *

It had been several days since Tate had come to her

rescue. Gigi was at the bakery, wiping down the counters aggressively as her thoughts stuck on the gorgeous Sinclair brother with the infuriating tendency to stick in her brain. *Why couldn't she stop thinking about him? Or the kiss?* Obviously, it hadn't meant anything to him considering not long after Brad had left, Tate also left because the rain had stopped and the water was starting to recede; everything was fine. He had swept in and saved her, basically, and then he had swept out. But he had left with a—she didn't want to say a chunk of her heart, but she had to admit to herself that he had touched something deep inside her that she had protected ferociously from everyone since Bill had walked out on her and before him, her dad. She was afraid to put her heart out there again in any way and because of that, she was destined to never have a happy ending if she continued to believe that all men left.

She had tried to dispel that when she'd opened her heart to Bill. But that had crashed and burned when he swept out of her life as quickly as he'd come into it.

She rubbed the rag over the counter harder, glad

for the peace that she had here for a few minutes. Because she knew Tate would follow the rest and he would not stay. But she could not stop thinking about him. *Did that make her a fool?*

The door opened and in walked Lulu, her first time in since arriving home from her honeymoon. Gigi brightened, seeing her.

"Lulu!" Gigi hurried around the counter and gave Lulu a hug. "It's so good to see you. I saw Brad the other night when he brought the extra sandbags that prevented my place from flooding. I was so glad to see him. Thanks to Tate, who thought to call him."

"I'm glad he called too. You know, you can always count on us if you need something. You should have called sooner."

"I know. I need to get better at asking for help."

Lulu gave her a look that said she better. Then she smiled. "Speaking of asking for help, that is one of the reasons I'm here. I dropped by to get my muffins but also to see if you're going to come help with the adoption day? I found the cutest little Goldendoodle at one of the shelters. They're bringing him and I really need your help with him."

Gigi looked at Lulu over the counter. She looked adorable today. Her hair was piled high on her head, bright-red and tussled, and her green eyes sparkled. "I just have to tell you that marriage looks good on you. You had a good time on your honeymoon, I guess?"

Lulu beamed. "I did. I did. I recommend a honeymoon to everyone. Even you, girl. I hope you've got somebody in mind. You have to get busy—we need to see a ring on your finger, too." Lulu beamed and waggled her eyebrows. "I'm hearing rumors about you and you-know-who."

Gigi thought about that and pushed the idea away. "Lulu, you know I'm not interested. I've got my life all settled out. And I don't know, I might be thinking about a puppy, so yes, you can count on me to help with the adoption day. But don't get your hopes up. I'm conflicted about getting an animal. I mean, that's a lot of responsibility."

"Gigi, give me a break. You are about the most responsible person I know. Look at you—taking over this bakery to help Rosie in the blink of an eye. You didn't even hesitate. And you're always here. Rosie can count on you for anything, so don't give me you're-not-responsible stuff. You help out with everything. Everybody in this town can count on you. You *need* a puppy."

"You think everyone needs a puppy." Gigi gave Lulu a blunt stare.

Lulu laughed. "Guilty as I can be. But you really do need a puppy and you're going to love this little Goldendoodle. Start thinking of a name."

Gigi went to fix Lulu her normal caramel mocha coffee. She looked over her shoulder as she was preparing it. "I'm going to help but I'm not sure yet if I'm going to get a puppy. So just be prepared. And if this Goldendoodle is as adorable as you're saying then I'm sure someone will take him, even if it's not me."

Lulu studied her with very frank eyes as she turned to set the coffee to go on the counter.

Ignoring the look, Gigi reached inside the cabinet and pulled out a cinnamon orange marmalade muffin. The delicious scent wafted up and filled her senses as she placed it into one of the cute little pink bags that said Bake My Day. "Do you need any extras today?"

Lulu grinned. "As a matter of fact, yes, I do. I think I need to go take one to that handsome fireman across the way at the fire station."

"Well, you know, he gets muffins delivered or he picks muffins up every morning for the firemen."

Lulu grinned. "Yes, I know he does but his wife can deliver him his very own muffins if she so desires."

Gigi laughed. She placed an extra muffin in the bag and then handed it to her across the counter. "I believe you're right. Muffins make a marriage last a lifetime."

"They bake my day," Lulu laughed, "and you will make my day when you help me and take this little Goldendoodle home. So mark my words...you are going to fall in love." Lulu headed toward the door, waving over her shoulder. "Ta-ta for now."

"See you later." As the door closed behind her friend, Gigi remained where she stood, her elbows resting on the glass counter and her hands clasped on top of it. *She was going to fall in love...* words that she would never let come true. But they were so tempting when she thought of Tate Sinclair. Halting her thoughts, she pulled away from the counter and returned to muffin baking. Lulu was one of the early customers as she was on her way to Lulu's Pet Paradise doggy daycare. The crowd had not arrived yet but they were coming, so Gigi had to be prepared.

She went to work but as she mixed muffin batter, her thoughts went to Tate. He hadn't been by, not since he'd helped save her home from flooding. Instead, others from the family had come by for Rosie's muffins. But there was no denying that she wished Tate would come by. She might not want a romance or a lifetime with him, something her inner voice kept telling her was wrong, but she did want to see him again.

Just see him. That was all. No hanky-panky involved. She just missed the man. It was a normal sentiment after he had done so much for her.

CHAPTER ELEVEN

Tate felt guilty ever since the night he had gone to Gigi's house and helped her and then kissed her. He had been flying high after that kiss. He never felt anything like that before and then Brad had stuck a needle in the balloon and popped all the good things he was feeling. Brad was right: there was something in him that couldn't be still. And what right did he have to come in here, to his hometown, and even think about having something with Gigi, who was clearly a hometown girl who didn't even hardly venture out of town? What had he been thinking?

He hadn't been thinking—that was the problem.

Brad had been man enough to tell it to him like he needed to hear it. He was glad that Gigi had someone like Brad looking out for her. Something about those pants that he'd worn that night bothered him. He wondered whether those had belonged to the guy who had hurt her. The guy who had swept into town, romanced her and then left. He wondered if this was the same guy who'd caused her to say she wouldn't date anyone like him.

He walked down the sidewalk from the beach, headed to the fire department. He was going to stop by and see Brad and the guys, and he saw that they were all over in the dog park. He could see Lulu's red hair and Brad standing there beside her. He watched them as he walked across the street toward everyone. The firehouse was across from the dog park and Lulu's Pet Paradise was on the opposite side of the dog park—practically straight across from the fire department. They had this area cornered and he had a feeling they could meet in that dog park whenever they wanted to for a little rendezvous. As he looked, Brad bent down and kissed his short wife's lips. They were different in size but Lulu's vibrant red hair—more orange than red, really—matched her temperament and she could keep up with the guy.

He opened the gate and walked in, seeing dogs everywhere. Only after he was inside the fence did he see all the signs and realize with all the people there that they were having a pet adoption day. He loved dogs but with his lifestyle and his schedule, having a pet was just not something that was practical, so he never had one. Didn't mean he didn't want one.

"Tate, come here. What are you doing?" Brad waved him over.

He weaved through the animals and the kids and the various people petting dogs that seemed to be on leashes and with tags on their collars.

"Hey, I didn't know y'all were having a—what is this…adoption day?"

Lulu smiled at him. "Yes, it is. Kind of taking on dogs that had no place—different shelters from the area bring pets out and we try to get them new owners. Get them happy homes. You want one?"

He held his hands up. "No, can't deal with one on my time schedule. It'd be hard dealing with them at the airports and if I left them, they'd be penned up too much or going to stay at a facility too much. I just don't think it's fair to a dog."

"Well, I admire your thought because that's kind of true. But I had to ask."

"I get it." He put his hands in his pockets and looked around the large dog park. As he looked, he spotted a familiar figure. She had her back to him but he knew Gigi anywhere. Guilt wrestled through him. He had pretty much left that night with a fairly odd exit. She probably wondered what had gone wrong or what had happened to him. She might not even be wondering about it at all. From what he knew, she was a loner; she probably was glad that he had left, especially after kissing her. But just thinking about that kiss sent a shiver through him of wanting to do it again, wanting to feel her in his arms and wanting to feel her pressed up against him. Yeah, he hadn't quit thinking about her. Something about that moment had just triggered something in him and he wasn't sure about it but Brad had straightened him out. Still, he knew he owed her an apology. No, owed her some kind of explanation.

"Anyway, I'm glad y'all are doing this but I need to go see Gigi for a minute."

"I think Gigi's going to adopt a dog." Lulu looked over in Gigi's direction. "That little Goldendoodle that she's petting...that puppy, it's been basically abandoned and Gigi's been thinking about a dog for a long time, I think, but she just wouldn't let herself have one. But I believe that little fella's going to steal her heart. I don't think she's going to be able to give him up. I saw the look in her eyes when she walked up and I handed him to her."

He looked at Lulu. "You have a way of matching dogs and people up?"

Brad laughed. "Does she? Yeah, I'd say she does. She's really good at what she does. So you better watch out. If she spots the one you need, you might be taking one home with you. Thankfully, she agrees with your assessment of your life—you are on the go a lot and you do move around a lot."

Brad raised an eyebrow and Tate got the hint; he was reminding him of their conversation.

"Yeah, I know. Anyway, I have to go see a gal. I think I owe her an apology."

Lulu looked at him with curiosity. "Oh, really? What would you have done to owe her an apology? From what I understand, you went out and helped her with a bad situation the night of the storm."

"Yeah, I did but I guess I didn't leave on exactly the best of terms. Anyway, it's okay. I just need to go tell her I'm sorry I left abruptly."

He headed that way, wondering why in the world he explained himself to them. Now they would know that he felt bad. He didn't really like people knowing his business like that but, well, he needed Brad to know that he understood he had boundaries now and he wasn't going to hurt Gigi.

She saw him coming before he reached her. He saw it in her face, which had been animated with excitement as she played with the Goldendoodle romping at her feet. Her shoulders stiffened and her lips—those beautiful, lush lips—flattened. *Oh yeah, she was not happy to see him.*

"Hi," he said. "How are you?"

"I'm fine. How are you?"

He looked at his feet and he looked at the little puppy. He bent down and the little puppy jumped at him. He grabbed it in his arms and petted it a few times before he looked up at her. "I'm feeling bad about the way I left after the storm. I think I owe you an explanation."

"No, you don't owe me anything. Thank you for coming to my rescue. Anyway, let's just leave it at that. You helped me out and I'm very grateful for that. You—we just kind of got a little carried away there for a moment but we're back. We're good. So no worries."

He didn't like the sound of that at all. But her eyes told him she didn't want to talk about it. They were too bright, as if she were forcing it; something about them didn't seem right. "Yeah, well, I don't know. Maybe you're right. But you know I've got things to do and in a month, I'll be gone."

"Yeah, I know. So all the more reason not to talk about that. I totally get it. So, anyway, please just let it go. I'm good."

He didn't know what else to say. He looked at the puppy and rubbed its ears. The puppy's tongue plopped out and his tail wagged. "He's a beauty. You gonna adopt him?" He stood up, holding the puppy. It wriggled in his arms. She lifted her hand and petted the puppy. Her hand briefly touched his wrist and fire shot through him. *Fire? What was that all about?*

"I think I am. I've been thinking a lot about getting an animal. I mean, I have that house and I have the yard—it seems a waste not to have a puppy like this that needs a home and me, not sharing mine with anything…this little baby Goldie, as I want to call him, is perfect. Lulu has been telling me about him for days. You know, Lulu's pretty aggressive when it comes to giving puppies out—or dogs. She has an affinity for older dogs but she said when this puppy came across her desk, she knew it was just right for me because she wanted me to have something that would be with me for a long time. Her thinking is exactly my thinking."

He studied her. He couldn't help think about the leaving thing again. Did Lulu also realize that there was something about people leaving that Gigi couldn't handle and a puppy would be around longer than an older dog? His gut tightened at the thought of Gigi being afraid of people leaving. All the more reason for him to stay back. The warning signals were going off but he had never in his life wanted to jump over a warning barrier and rush forward like he did right now.

* * *

"Tate, maybe you need to adopt that puppy." Gigi needed to say something because looking at Tate, gorgeous and holding that adorable puppy, just made her heart melt. She did not need her heart melting anymore where this man was concerned. She was in danger and she knew it. She'd tried so hard and yet one kiss—one lousy, amazing, unbelievable kiss—had set her back eons. But still, she was trying to hold firm. She could only get hurt at the end of this.

"I don't know—I heard you were adopting this baby."

"Let me guess…you heard that from Lulu. She's

been pushing this, as you say, baby on me and I have to say I'm thinking about it. I don't know…it might be nice to come home to something every evening." *Why had she said that? Why had she let him see inside her head?* Yes, she definitely had been thinking about taking the puppy home, just because he had brought home her loneliness. She'd been fine until Tate had come into town and messed with her contentment. Yes, it might have been a forced contentment but still, she had settled and she had been fine and now she wasn't. She could deny it all she wanted but she wasn't okay. But now all she wanted to do was fling herself into the man's arms and kiss the daylights out of him, or beg him to kiss the daylights out of her. This was not healthy thinking.

Not healthy at all.

Not to her.

Instead, she reached for the puppy. She needed to hold the puppy; she did not need to look at him holding the puppy any longer. As she tried to take the puppy from him, she had to step close to him. She smelled the delicious scent of his cologne and it only took her back to that moment when she was engulfed in his arms and he was kissing her. *Oh my gosh, this was just too terrible.* Her eyes met his and she got her arms around the puppy and yet he hadn't let go. In that brief, shocking, lightning strike of an instant, she saw in his eyes the same need she felt in herself. If she didn't see it, then she was lying to herself. But every molecule in her body went into a tailspin. Her knees melted, and if she hadn't been hanging on to the puppy and he hadn't still been hanging onto it too, she probably would have just melted right there into a puddle.

"Gigi, are you seriously doing okay? I am really sorry." He said the words low and gentle and they seeped through her like honey pouring over her—warm, lovely, delicious honey.

She just paused, entangled there with the puppy and him, wanting to lean forward so badly and kiss his gorgeous, sweet-talking lips. *They are not sweet-talking,* she told herself; *they are not sweet-talking. They're leaving lips; they're going to leave.*

"Can you talk to me?" He leaned forward just a little bit, earnestness edging his words.

"I'm confused." It was the only thing she could say. It was an honest answer—she was so confused.

"To be honest, so am I. I know I don't need to be starting something with you. I know I'm not good for you. I know you're content, and I know that you're settled. And I know you were hurt by your last boyfriend leaving you. I know all of this and I understand you're afraid to trust somebody like me, somebody whose job takes them away all the time. But Gigi, even knowing that, I just can't get you off my mind."

Her breath halted in her lungs. *He was being honest too. They were being honest with each other.* Their gazes held. She wanted to just dive into those beautiful eyes of his. She felt bad judging him by the other men in her life who had hurt her.

She tipped her head and let out a trembling breath, a breath she'd been holding as he spoke. "Well, what do we do? I hate the sound of that question. It sounds like I'm judging you and I also sound so vulnerable. Like such a victim and I hate all of this. I don't normally let people see my vulnerability. And yet, I let my guard down and let you see it all." She stared, realizing she had done it again, laid everything out there, just bared her soul to him again. Her eyes probably told everything.

His expression was intense as if he was trying hard to understand. She wanted him to understand.

He inhaled and touched her cheek, brushing his thumb across her skin, making her long to move closer to him. "Maybe we're starting at a good place right now," he said. "We're both being honest. I've been denying it ever since that night I kissed you. I've been denying it ever since that night you asked me to get you out of that wedding reception. There is something here and I can't stop myself from wanting to find out what it is. But I don't want you to do anything you don't want to do."

She smiled as the puppy licked her on the chin, reminding her that the puppy was still in her arms and they were still connected right here in the middle of the dog park with everyone who could possibly be watching probably riveted to them. "I want to say no, I don't want to do this. I'm scared. And I wouldn't ever admit that to anyone but it's true. And yet, I want to see you. And I have to warn you that right now I have a feeling everyone's watching us." To her surprise, she felt him let go of the puppy with one arm and it snaked around her waist.

He tugged her closer. "Then let them see this." And then his hand slipped from her cheek to the base of her neck and he tugged her forward and he kissed her.

CHAPTER TWELVE

"When you two stop that kissing, I've got those dogs over here that you promised you'd get baths for, Gigi." Lila's voice broke into Tate's spinning world.

With much effort, he stopped kissing Gigi. "Uh, hey there, Ms. Peabody. You have interesting timing."

Lila giggled mischievously. "I've always been told that. Now I'm thinking that maybe you could help Gigi here bathe Maddog over there."

"Maddog? Who would bring a dog to an adoption with a name like Maddog?"

"He's just a little ole baby. It's kind of a joke. He's as sweet as they come but he is a big fella, so I think it would be really nice for you to help her. Here, let me take this sweet puppy off your hands while you bathe Maddog. I'll keep him safe," she said, as Gigi, wearing a dazed look so like the one she'd had the night of the storm when he'd kissed her, watched as Lila pulled the puppy from her arms.

Longing for the puppy replaced the dazed expression, and he was transfixed as he watched her relinquish the puppy. Her expression was so readable that he wondered whether she even knew how much she wanted to keep the Goldendoodle puppy.

His thoughts flew straight back to that night in her kitchen when he'd kissed her. Gigi looked pretty dazed after the kiss he had given her. He was dazed himself. There was some chemistry like nobody's business going on between them. If there was ever anybody who had a stronger connection, he didn't know how. "What do you say—you want to help her? I'm willing."

Gigi took a breath as if to get her bearings and

nodded. "That'd be great. Let's go. But I promise you, Maddog's not real fond of men."

"I just don't think y'all have brought a dangerous dog up here. Besides, if he's going to be a bad dog, then I'm going to be over there to protect you. I think you two have something up your sleeves."

They both were smiling; they turned and he followed them. They walked across the dog park to the bathing area that had been set up. There was an enclosure for people to get inside with the dog to let them play instead of letting them run. And in the enclosures were several dogs, he guessed, waiting to get baths. Why anybody would bring a dog in need of a bath up to an adoption he wasn't sure, but then again, with the way he traveled, he had never been to an adoption before. Maybe this was normal.

Gigi looked in the pen where several dogs were running around. Over in the corner sat a very hairy, very big, black dog.

Lila pointed at it and winked. "There's Maddog. He's all y'alls. Yours."

Lulu waved from where she was helping a little boy and a mother with a dog. "I promise you he's a sweetheart. I don't know why they gave him that name. I think we're going to change it because it scares everybody off. Don't be afraid."

Gigi shrugged as Lila walked away, smiling. "They promise me he's a great dog. But nobody was willing to give him a bath so I volunteered. With all that hair, he gets miserable on a hot day."

"Gigi, I have figured out that when nobody else will do something or if somebody else needs something, you just jump right in there and take care of it. Maybe this is one time you shouldn't have done that."

She cocked her head to the side and put her hands on her hips. "Lulu needed help. And I am not about to tell her no."

"Well, all right. So let me ask you this: since you don't have a dog and I don't have a dog, do you know how to give a dog a bath?"

* * *

Gigi stared at Tate. "How hard can it be to give a dog a bath?"

He hitched his brows and nodded toward Maddog. "One that big and hairy has got to be a complication. I'm just asking."

"Are you scared? Mr. Big Adventurer. You'll jump off mountains and fly over buildings but you don't want to bathe a big ole hairy dog?"

He laughed. "I'll dive in there and bathe that dog. I'm just asking if you know any tips." He winked at her.

Oh, she liked that wink. She couldn't get used to that, that's for sure. She was letting herself get in too deep. "All right, well, I'll be in there with you. Let's go. We're supposed to use that big pan over there." She pointed toward a big wash bucket.

"I don't think they call that a pan. I think they call that a barrel or something. As long as they have a water hose with a good sprayer and a lot of shampoo, I think we'll be okay."

She wasn't so sure about that the closer she got to Maddog. The big ole dog looked at her with soulful eyes. "Hi there, big fella, you look lonely over here. Nobody petting you?"

She reached out and let the dog sniff her hand. He licked it. "Well, that was saying hello in an easy manner. I believe someone has definitely given you the wrong name. Who would do such a thing?"

Tate held his hand out and the dog licked it, too, and laid his head on his hand. "Um, well, I think you might be right. He is definitely a softy."

"And it looks like he likes you."

Tate took his hand and rubbed the dog's head. The big ole dog looked like he was in heaven. "Come on, let's get this leash right here and we'll take him over there."

Gigi reached for the biggest leash that was hooked to the fence and grabbed it, then clicked it onto his collar. To her surprise, the big dog stood up and walked beside her as though he'd been doing it all his life. She looked at Tate. "This is unbelievable. He acts like he's used to this. I wonder what his story is."

Tate looked conflicted too. "I don't know but somebody has to know. We'll have to ask Lulu what it is. Surely she'll know."

They got the dog over there to the bathing barrel, as she decided to call it. Maddog wasn't as cooperative about getting into the wash bucket as he was walking with the leash, so Tate grabbed him gently around his whole body, lifted him up and placed him ever so slowly in the center of the galvanized basin. They were very glad that the dog seemed cooperative. Gigi got a water hose and turned it on and that's when they saw Maddog's eyes get a little alarmed. They widened and rolled back in the back of his head a little bit. Tate grabbed hold of his collar easily, just in case he decided to bolt. And just in case he had any kind of aggression, he didn't want him getting away into the group, she assumed.

"I'm going to hold him for right now, just until we know he's okay. I don't want you getting bit."

Aw, he was looking out for her. Gigi's heart melted a little bit. "Thank you. I think he's just afraid, though."

She took the water hose and very carefully placed it on the dog. The water was warmed by the water hose being in the sun but she knew cold water was coming. Sure enough, soon as that colder water hit him, he shivered. But he stood his ground and Tate held onto the collar. She laughed and smiled at Tate; Tate smiled back at her. He reached over to the table and picked up a big bottle of shampoo and squirted it all over Maddog's black, furry coat. Gigi put the water hose down and then dug her fingers into the mass of hair and began to scrub. As she scrubbed on all that hair, the suds from the shampoo began to multiply. And multiply and multiply. She looked at Tate. His eyes were starting to get a little wide, too. Maddog was beginning to look like a big white fluffy marshmallow.

"I think maybe I put too much shampoo on him."

"I think you might be right. I wasn't really paying attention when you started squirting on there but yes, with all this hair, it's going to take us forever to rinse him off. But I'm digging deep. I've got to get down to his skin, so I just got to keep on going."

"Well, I feel bad just holding his collar. Here, I'll

hold with this one hand and rub with the other." He reached in and started digging in with his hand down into the hair, reaching to the skin—she could tell by the fact that his arm disappeared up to past his wrist, just like hers, and then past his elbows with the suds getting so big.

"Well, this is an adventure."

He grinned. *Oh, she loved that grin.* Her heart tilted over and fell out right there in her chest. Yup, she was in major, major trouble.

"Thanks for helping me," she said over the suds growing between them. He lifted his hand out of the suds and tapped her nose with some; she giggled and wiped it away with her elbow. "No, no, let's don't start that. We'll get into a suds fight, which might be kind of fun but we'll disturb the dog and we don't need to scare him."

"Much as I'm tempted, I think you're right. So for now you're safe. But I'll have to figure out another way to get you back."

"Get me back for what?"

"Getting me into this."

"Well then, I guess that's fine because I don't regret it."

"Me either. Now, I guess get that water hose and let's see if we can start rinsing this off because it could take all day and you know we probably need to leave at some point. And if you're going to adopt that Goldendoodle over there—which she really did look like she belonged to you—then you'll need time to fill the paperwork out and everything."

Gigi looked at Maddog. "I wonder who's going to adopt this big boy. He's so big I can't even imagine."

"I don't know but he's pretty good-sized. He's probably too big for you."

"Actually, you're right—the little doodle will do me much better. She's going to grow to be a bigger dog than she is now. But he was sitting over there, lonely, and nobody was like even looking at him. I wonder if it's just his name scaring them off or the fact that he's so big."

"Somebody surely will come out of the woodwork and adopt him. Mark my words, we're going to give him this bath and he's going to be beautiful. We'll comb him down, get his hair looking prettier than it was—spruce him up. I bet he finds a new owner who's going to love him and give him baths all the time. It's such a fun treat."

She laughed. They finished washing him and she accidentally squirted Tate a few times as she used the water hose to rinse the dog off.

"Hey, I think you did that on purpose."

"I'll never tell. I've just got a terrible, terrible aim."

"Yeah…I think you tell white lies, too."

Yeah, she thought to herself; *little white lies like she wasn't falling for Tate Sinclair when in truth, she had already fallen.*

* * *

"So, how's it going? With Tate?" Rosie asked a week after the dog adoption. Rosie was doing better and Erin had brought her in to have coffee and muffins and visit with all the customers as they came in. Of course, all the girls were there: Lila, Doreen, Birdie, and Mami.

Rosie smiled like a Cheshire cat, the little minx. She knew that asking that question was going to get the gals all riled up because they had been drilling her and asking questions all week.

She and Tate had been seeing a lot of each other over the last week. She was being brave; she was putting herself out there.

She had adopted Goldie and thankfully, just like Tate had predicted, once they got Maddog spruced up and all combed and shiny handsome, people had started to come over and visit with him. He was a hit and had been snapped up really quickly. The man was good with his instincts. She just hoped she was good with hers. It would be a first.

He was actually at Adam's office today, hopefully getting his boot removed from his ankle. She knew he was so ready to get rid of the thing. And she was, too. He was a guy who didn't need to be in something like that and it just wasn't right, so she couldn't wait for him to have the boot off and get around like himself again. In the back of her mind, she also worried once he had the boot off, there was nothing holding him here in Sunset Bay. She wasn't thinking about that right now. "Things are good. You know that, Rosie."

"I know but it's fun asking you because I just think you look so happy and that makes me happy. Right, girls?"

The ladies all smiled and lifted their mugs of coffee in the air.

"We'll toast to that," Birdie said. "I never realized you weren't happy. You're just always so perky but now, since I've seen you with Tate, you're just beaming like sunshine and I want to see that from here on out."

Lila smiled. "Me and old Maddog, we did pretty good that day at the adoption, I think. That big ole dog—he's such a sweetheart. I knew he would help you two get in the suds together."

Gigi looked at Lila. "What did you say?"

Lila giggled. "I've had big dogs before and I know exactly how hard they are to bathe. All that big, thick hair—you got to get down and close when you're scrubbing on them and I just knew you two would have to bond over that, you know."

Gigi shook her head at the little stinker.

Mami reached out and tapped her arm. "That is one good-looking man, darling. Believe me, I haven't got to enjoy him jogging down the beach since his leg's messed up but I'm always on the beach when I know he's in town because he does look good without his shirt on. So there's a plus right there. I'm glad you got him."

She did not have him; they were all a little bit confused about that. She had him for a little while and she was just having to talk herself into being content with that. She was resigned to the fact that he would probably leave but she wasn't going to think about that.

Doreen hadn't said anything but she was pink. That always meant she was thinking something.

"Doreen, you sure are quiet over there. What's on your mind? I know something's on your mind. Everybody else is speaking, so you might as well too."

"I was just thinking how romantic it is. You've been helping Rosie out so much and you're just always helping everybody out and I'm just glad you have somebody now."

That did it. She fought off telling them that she didn't have him but this was Doreen and she didn't want to make Doreen feel bad. "Thank you but y'all, you know he's a very active guy—he comes and goes. So I'm just enjoying him while he's here."

"Sometimes the ones who get their going out early are the ones who stick around in the end. I'm not saying that guys don't get their running—I mean, you know what I'm saying." Doreen turned pinker.

Actually, Gigi didn't know what Doreen was trying to say. But she wasn't going to question Doreen because she was already flustered enough, poor gal. She was so shy and flustered that Gigi just let that go.

"Well, y'all sit here and visit. I'm going to go check on the muffins. It might be time to put some new ones in."

They protested as she walked away but she couldn't help it; she needed a break. Thankfully, the doors opened and more customers came in, so she had something to keep her busy. When the door jangled after she had watched the three customers leave after she filled their orders, she saw a very attractive, beautiful man walk in the door. Her heart turned over and her breath caught in her throat. He strode into the bakery with the gait of a man who had healed, strong limbs. He was not wearing the dreaded boot.

He stopped halfway into the room, put his hands on his lean hips, and smiled at her. "I am a free man. And just in time. What do you think?"

She smiled at him. She couldn't help herself; she went around the counter and walked up to him and gave him the once-over. She couldn't help teasing him. "Looks like you're all healed up. You look better than ever." And he did.

"I'll second that," Mami said. The ladies behind him giggled and laughed and more words were tossed out to make him grin.

He turned and looked at the ladies behind him. "Well, you little sneakers, y'all are sitting over there— I didn't even see y'all."

"Could it be because you only have eyes for my employee?" Rosie laughed.

"Well, Rosie, you might be on to something right

there."

"Might be?" Rosie asked.

Tate looked at her, his eyes assessing and serious. "Yeah, I wouldn't say might. You're right."

Okay, this was getting a little too serious and a little too public. "Tate, could I see you in the back?"

She took his hand and didn't wait for him to answer her as she led him into the back of the bakery. Everybody was watching her. She was not used to being the object of everyone's attention. She got him into the back and pulled him all the way back by the freezer at the far wall so no one could hear their conversation. She was about to say something but before she could, Tate cupped her face between his hands and lowered his mouth to hers. He took her breath away, melted her knees, and caused all kinds of chaos inside her. She was a goner. She just had to pray that he wasn't leaving.

When he finished kissing her breathless, he pulled back and smiled at her. "Hello."

"Hi," she breathed—barely, considering she was about to faint.

"I have plans for us this evening. Now that I can get around without that dang boot, I'm going to fix you a romantic dinner at my place. Okay?"

"Okay. You cook?"

"Yes, I do. Not that much but I can get us something to eat. Moonlight dinner on the deck, the sound of the seagulls in the surf…can't get any better than that with a beautiful woman sitting across from me or beside me or in my arms. Yeah, now that I don't have the boot on, I can move around and I don't know…I just feel like doing something special for you, Gigi."

"Okay. I can't say no to that."

"All right then, I'll see you about seven. Does that give you time? Can you drive yourself over?"

"I can do that. And yes—seven, I'll be there. Can I bring anything?"

"Just your beautiful self."

And with that, he turned and strode purposefully out of the storeroom, around the bakery cases, and then out of her sight from where she remained standing at the back of the storeroom near the freezer. Reaching for the door, she opened it and let the cold air blast her. She needed something to get her brain functioning again and to get the hot flashes to leave. She definitely did not want to walk back out there with pink cheeks, which she knew she had.

Could she let herself be happy? She wanted to. She wanted to so much.

CHAPTER THIRTEEN

Tate was in the middle of fixing dinner and watching the clock in anticipation for when Gigi would get to the beach house. He had enjoyed seeing her this week; it had been great. And it had sent conflicting emotions through him but he knew he didn't want her to not know how serious he was. So he decided that tonight he was going to tell her just what she meant to him.

His phone rang but he didn't answer it when he saw that it was his agent. *How did Freddy know the exact wrong moments to call him?* He let it go to voicemail. He had a lot of thinking to do.

The doorbell rang and he went to answer it. Gigi looked stunning when he opened the door. She had a blue sundress on and her hair hung softly around her shoulders. *He could get used to seeing her every day of her life.* The strong sentiment rocked him. But he knew it was true. He was falling for her and there was nothing he could do about it. That's why they needed to have a talk. His job—his lifestyle—took him away and though she had never completely told him what the problem was, he knew she had a problem with that. He needed to find out what that was and how deep it ran tonight.

"Come in. You are stunning."

"Thanks. I decided to put a dress on tonight, not jeans or shorts. I don't often dress up."

"I'll take you any way you want to dress, but I have to say, I like that blue dress."

She blushed beautifully. His heart just ached to give her everything she ever wanted. He had never felt that way about anybody. He wanted to know what things she dreamed of. Was there anything special in her life that she wanted or needed? He wanted to be the man to give it to her. He kind of understood where his brothers were coming from now.

"Come back here. We'll get the meal started before the sun gets ready to set. It's going to be a beautiful night."

They went into the kitchen and as they talked about her day and the girls teasing her at work and how glad he was to have his boot off, they laughed and just enjoyed themselves. When the steaks were ready, he carried the plates out to the deck table that he had already set and put them on the table. He pulled her chair out for her and she looked at him as if he had lost his mind. "Don't look at me like that. I can pull a chair out for a lady."

"Thank you. It's been awhile since anyone did that."

He took a deep breath and as she scooted the chair in, he sat down in his chair. "I'm hoping to set you on a new path so you'll forget the guy who caused you to stop dating anyone."

He reached for her hand and ran his thumb over

the soft skin of her wrist. "I hope you know how much I've enjoyed getting to know you. And how special I think you are. And I hope you know I'm not that guy who hurt you."

She started to say something, then stopped, looked out at the ocean and then looked back at him. "I thought we were coming here to enjoy a nice meal?"

"We are, but I think our relationship has progressed to the point where we could dig deeper. I want to understand you better."

"Tate, what's there to understand? Bill loved to travel. I met him—we started dating. He told me he was ready to settle down, and I fell for that, fell for him...it never dawned on me that he would leave. I thought we were going to get engaged; instead, he left me and went on his adventure."

"I'm not him. All men don't leave and never come back."

"Not in my life."

"What does that mean?"

"Tate, I've learned in my life that the men I love leave and they don't ever come back. My dad did it first."

"What?"

"Yeah, he abandoned me and my mom. He left my junior year in high school, and my mom and I were in pretty bad shape. He cleaned out the bank account. We made it but it was hard. **Mom and I pulled together and both worked extra in order to pay the bills, to keep the house...he hadn't paid the note in months. I just couldn't understand how the man I had loved could do that. We were both shocked and grieved at his walking away.**"

He felt sick. "I didn't know. That was terrible, really awful. I'm sorry."

Her eyes were dull. "It is what it is. Life isn't perfect, we play the cards we're dealt. Right?"

"That still doesn't make it right. Maybe I shouldn't have brought all that up, but Gigi, you can trust me." He was an idiot—yup, just an idiot. He had planned this meal and now he had her talking and it was pretty depressing. Depressing in the fact that she was never going to go along with his lifestyle. He could only imagine he'd be gone and she'd be here and she'd think he wasn't coming back. Basically, what she said he would do.

She picked up her fork and took a bite of her stuffed flounder. "This is delicious. You know, it would've been more romantic if we hadn't had that conversation we just had."

"Yeah, well, I'm living and learning. Definitely not the smartest move I've ever made." He put his fork down. "Look, Gigi, I'm going to be leaving, but I'm coming back. My job takes me away but I come back."

She set her fork down and put her hands in her lap. "But you don't come back for long. You stop in for a visit and then you're gone again. And I told myself ever since I started wanting to see you and get involved with you that I was being a fool. Because I knew you have this want and need inside you—you love what you do and you're really good at it. I couldn't hold a guy like you here. I knew that. And then I did it anyway. So, Tate, I came into this with my eyes wide open. And, you know, we've really only been dating for a week. Well, we've been seeing each other off and on but not really dating, so it's not long."

"It's long enough, Gigi—it's long enough for me to know that I don't want to lose you. And we need to find a way to make this work."

Her lips trembled. "I don't see how it could work. I'm not going to be satisfied to see you two or three days out of every three or six months. How many times last year did you come to town?"

"I came a couple of days at a time—probably a handful of times. But, Gigi, I didn't have anyone here other than my family. I didn't have anyone special to come back to. Yeah, I love my family but my career...my life—it wasn't here. But you're here now and I'll be back more." It sounded stupid, even to him. *What kind of life was that?* She'd just be hanging around here. *What had he done?*

She looked conflicted. She took a deep breath and then placed her napkin on the table. "Tate, I don't know why we're doing this but it's probably time. If there's no reason for us to keep this up, I should know now. I can't do this. You did right bringing me here and telling me this. I just got carried away. It's only a week—we can put it behind us and move on." She stood.

He stood. "I don't want to go on. I don't want it to stop."

"Tate, I can't do this. I waited for my dad to come back for years and my mom did too. I didn't have to wait on Bill—I knew he wasn't coming back. He chose something more dazzling than me. I'm boring and I know it. I like it that way."

"Gigi, come on—give this a chance. We can figure this out. You can come with me."

She laughed. "My job is here—my life is here."

"We can make our home base here. You write— remember, you got all those books you can send in. You can go on the road with me. Think how great it would be."

"Tate, I'm not a traveler. I don't want to live out of a suitcase. I like my life. I like being settled. I like having a place of my own. I don't…I don't want to do that."

He hadn't thought about that. He was grasping at straws. "Gigi, I'm falling in love with you. Doesn't that count for anything?"

A tear trailed out of her eye. She wiped it away and sniffed. "It's easier this way. Believe me, nearly getting to the altar and then instead watching him walk away is so much harder."

She turned and walked toward the door. He followed her. "Wait. You can't just leave."

"Tate, when are you leaving?"

He raked a hand through his hair. "I have a job that starts in two days. That's why I wanted to talk to you." He knew that's why his agent had been calling; they were supposed to discuss his leaving, wanting to make sure his leg was okay.

"And I hope you have a wonderful time. It's been great."

She turned and walked through the door.

He just stood there, wondering what had happened.

* * *

Gigi cried when she got in her car. She had known this was coming. Known he was going to leave. But to expect or think that she could just wait around for him? She couldn't understand that. She couldn't do it. She wiped the tears out of her eyes as she drove. He hadn't been thinking either, obviously, or he wouldn't even have broached that subject. Had he thought all along that she would do that?

It seemed as if that was all she'd ever done. She still remembered in high school when she and her mom were just in limbo, waiting and hoping that her dad would come to his senses and come home. But no, he never did. She'd sworn that she would never ever let a man rip out her heart again, and then she'd let her guard down and given her heart to Bill. And just like her daddy, he had left. She couldn't do that again. She'd said you played the cards you were dealt but that didn't mean you kept playing off the same deck. No, she couldn't let herself fall for a guy who might leave too.

She would just go home and cuddle with Goldie and that would be it. Goldie was going to be the only thing she gave her heart to ever again. She reached her driveway, turned in too quickly, ran over the curb then braked really hard, and came to a jolting halt. She put the car in park, put her hands on the wheel, and leaned her head forward and let the tears come.

Behind her, lights blared, filling the car. She lifted her head and looked behind her at the two lights on high beam and the vehicle pulled in halfway behind her. Someone was yanking her door open. And she looked to find Tate looking at her with a fierce expression on his face.

"You can't just run away like that. Come on, get out of there." He took her hands and pulled her out of the car.

She wiped her face as best she could on her shoulder, shrugging to get it up. There was no hiding her tears, though. "What are you doing, Tate?"

"I'm coming after the woman I love."

"Tate, I cannot do what you are asking me to do. I can't."

He clung to her hands. His warmth, his energy flowed through her but she fought back against it, closing her heart.

"Then I'll do whatever you need me to do."

"No. I don't want you to do anything. You have your life and I have mine. We have two different wants and needs out of this world. We knew that from the beginning. We should've never let this go this far. I don't know what I was thinking. Obviously I wasn't thinking. And neither were you, Tate. I'm just a liability. You love what you do. Just look how energized you are since you got that boot off your foot. You're like a whole new person. You've got enough energy for like twenty people and you already have a job lined up. I'm not...I don't want...I can't do this. So just please let me end it now before I invest any more of my heart because I'm not going to do that. Now go. And do your thing. And have a good life, okay?"

She saw his stunned expression and her heart ached. She wanted to throw herself into his arms but instead she tore her hands from his and then ran for her door. When she got inside, she closed it behind her. She leaned against it, just as her legs gave out and she sank down to sit on the floor. Goldie came running and dove into her lap with snuggles and wiggles and love.

She wrapped her arms around her puppy and cuddled him to her heart.

And ignored Tate on the other side of the door, asking her to open the door.

* * *

"You look like heck," Brad said the next morning as he and Jonah and Adam met him down at the dock. He had called an emergency meeting of the minds.

"Brad's right. I thought you were really happy," Jonah said. "I thought you and Gigi had something. Is that what this is about? Did something happen?"

Adam was studying him but didn't say anything.

Tate nodded and raked a hand through his hair that was probably already overworked from his hands running through it so many times in frustration as he had paced his living room most of the night. "She broke it off. She won't open her door. She won't answer her phone. I've left messages until her mailbox is full. She made it clear she can't live my lifestyle. And she doesn't even want to talk about making this my home base and traveling out from here. I'm kind of at a loss. And now that my ankle is well, they've asked me to get back to the movie set. Then I've got that jump off a mountain for a commercial. I've got to go. And I don't know what to do. I've never been in any situation like this before."

Adam leaned forward, propped his elbows on his knees, and cupped his hands together. His other brothers were thinking also, as if they didn't want to say anything. Adam gave him a point-blank stare. "Tate, I hate to tell you this but this relationship isn't all about you. If that's something she can't do, then she can't do it."

"A relationship is give-and-take," Jonah said. "You've got to support her and she's got to support you."

"Yeah. They're right," Brad said. "Lulu and I, we learned early on that we have to trust each other. And I think that maybe Gigi has some trust issues. Remember, I told you something's holding her back."

He let out a long sigh. "Yeah, you're right, it is. Okay, remember in high school how she was different the last year or two? I mean, I never really knew her that well because she wasn't in my grade, but Jonah, she was in yours. Do you remember if she was quieter? I was graduating her junior year and I just barely remember that she dropped out of a bunch of stuff. I had to think about it a lot last night. She had been fairly active. She liked drama club—remember that?— and I think she played on the softball team with Erin and Cassie. And then she was just gone. I remember them saying something about they were going to the finals that year and she dropped out all of a sudden."

Brad sat up. "Yeah, I remember that."

Jonah looked really thoughtful. "I do remember that she got quieter and she started working. And I think she worked a couple of jobs."

Adam's face grew sympathetic. "What happened that year?"

"Her dad left. He just ran off and left them in a lot of debt—a pretty big mess. And they were close to losing the house. And not only had they lost him, but they had to cover all the debt to save the house. Her mom just kind of checked out for a while, so she had a

193

lot on her plate. She's a fighter but she doesn't trust men anymore, you know. She waited for her dad. Her mom never gave up on waiting for her dad. I think Gigi finally did and she moved away. She finally fell in love and believed he was going to marry her but he left her and broke her heart."

"Oh, wow," Jonah said.

"Yeah, it was bad. Really tore her up. And then she moved back here and that's been it. And then I come along and in a whirlwind, just kind of took her by surprise. And I..." He hung his head, his heart aching. His thoughts rolled over and over with what an idiot he was. He sighed and looked up at his brothers, who were all watching him expectantly. "I just barreled into her life and kind of ignored all the warnings she was giving me. I just kind of went crazy. I had never felt like that before and now I've hurt her. I guess I just expected that she would go with me or wait here for me."

"And she won't?"

"She won't. She barely let me talk about it, and then she left and shut me out. So, I'm going to go. I brought you out here to ask your advice and then to tell you...I mean, I think what I'm going to do is I'm going to go and I'm going to give her some time. Then I'll come back and see how she feels."

Brad grimaced. "I don't know if that's a good idea. I mean, I told you that you might be hurting her more. If you're not going to be able to fix it, then maybe you just need to let her go."

"Seriously?" He looked at his brothers and they all nodded. "I just don't want to do that."

Jonah stood and put a hand on his shoulder. "I learned with Summer that hurt can go really deep. And we were so blessed, growing up. You know we had that great life. Still do. But there are hurts sometimes that we don't understand. And I did...I had to give Summer a little bit of time, so do what you've got to do. And while you're gone, I'll look in on her. I'll watch out for her. And Summer will help, too. I think all of us will."

"Yeah, me and Lulu will."

Adam waved his hand. "You know Rosie and I will, and we'll let Erin in on it. Cassie's too busy—

she's not here half the time either, so we won't worry her with it. Yeah, you've got to do your job. But sometimes, Tate, your dreams change. Maybe you should give that a thought. My dreams changed and I have never looked back."

"Thanks, guys. I've got a lot to think about. All right, thank y'all for doing that. I'll be in touch. I'm not sure when I'll be back. With this ankle having pulled me back, they held that spot open on that film as long as they could. It's right up against my jump so it's going to be a little while…maybe a month."

"We've got your back. And Gigi's."

"Okay then, I'll go. I've got to stop by and tell Mom and Dad bye then head out. But don't tell them any of this—it's just between us, okay?"

"We totally have your back on that." Brad grimaced. "It's going to be hard. Anyway, they're going to get the picture. We're going to have to live with all of Mom's questions but we'll do our best. You be safe. Watch out for those ankles."

"Yeah, I will." And then he walked down the dock and headed back to his life.

CHAPTER FOURTEEN

Gigi walked along the beach. Goldie ran up ahead of her, chasing a seagull and yapping as she went. She was getting bigger. Puppies could grow fast in the five weeks since she had adopted her sweetie. She breathed in deep and let the peace of the morning ease through her. She had been struggling some in the month since Tate had left. But she had an iron will and she had put it into action. She started doing affirmations in her morning prayers; she had started walking. Rosie had hired two new people to help out at the bakery, giving her some time off, and she realized it was much-needed time off.

Tate had told her that she was always there for people and she had been. She enjoyed what she did but she also hadn't realized that she really had no life outside of her work. She had finally sat down and looked at her writing and realized that he was right: she didn't just not take risks in love—she didn't take risks at all. She had sent out some query letters to publishers. And she had also reached out to Nash, Erin's husband. He was a phenomenon in the traditional publishing world and she got his advice on how to approach that end of publishing.

She had also been hooked up with Trent Sinclair's wife, Lilly. Lilly was also a phenomenon but in the world of independent publishing and she had gotten advice on how to do that from her. She was juggling between the two, trying to decide what she wanted to do. She knew she could go the indie route and she was thinking that was probably what she was going to do, but she knew that before she did that, she had to force herself to take the risk and accept rejection from traditional publishing. It was something she just had to make herself do.

Today, she had a letter in her pocket. She was going to read it; she was going to step out and take that chance. She hadn't just sent one query letter out—she had sent several—but just the act of putting the letters in the email and pushing Send had about given her a nervous breakdown. But once she'd done it, something in her head clicked with pride. She had been proud of herself because she had gone out on that ledge and stepped out on faith. Actually, she had stepped out with a push from Tate, his words of truth to her.

She missed him. She wouldn't think about that. No, she was not going to think about that at all. He had been gone a month; he had sent her messages and emails that she hadn't opened. She couldn't. She was grateful that he had pushed her but she was getting stronger and she wasn't going to look back.

She wasn't going to wait but, one day, she would take a chance on someone who was more like her. Yes, she was managing a risk on that one but she couldn't help it; it was a different story than sending her book out to publishers. This was still dealing with her heart and she just had to manage that. To some point, anyway. She knew his brothers and his sister and his sisters-in-law had all been looking out for her. They all checked on her and invited her over, and the girls did, too—Mami and Birdie. It was so obvious how everybody had gathered around and really shown her that she wasn't as alone as she thought she was. Yeah, they were connected to her because of Tate but she really appreciated them.

Suddenly, Goldie turned and took off running, back across the sand as fast as her legs would carry her. She was bounding across the sand.

"Goldie, come back." Alarm rang through Gigi and she took off running across the soft white sugar sand, which wasn't easy to do. Her feet buried in the deep sand. One instant she was running after her puppy, and the next she landed face-first in the sand.

"Looks like you're in a predicament."

Her heart clutched and then pounded fiercely at his voice. She looked up from the sand and shook her face to get it off her. There he was, standing in front of her, smiling and holding Goldie in his big, amazing arms. "Tate—you're back."

He bent down in front of her, ran a hand over Goldie's head, smiled at her, and then set her down. "Yeah, I am. Here—let me help you up." He reached down and took her hands and then gently pulled her so that she was standing. "How are you? Haven't gotten your dresses hung up in any bathroom doors lately, have you?"

Her knees weren't going to hold her up if he let go of her hands. Thankfully, he hadn't let go yet. "No, not lately but I haven't had any weddings to go to. Summer and Jonah's isn't until next month."

He just stared at her and her heart pounded. She blinked back emotion that tried to well up in her. *She would not cry.* She would keep this friendly, not personal. But the way he was looking at her made it really hard. "Tate, this…" she murmured and pulled on her hands.

He did not let go. "Gigi, why haven't you answered my messages?"

"Because I told you we needed to end it and just dragging it on—I couldn't do that."

"But I might have needed to say something important."

"I can't do this. I've come a long way since you've been gone."

"Yeah, I heard through the grapevine. I hear you are doing more writing."

She had actually told people that she was trying to be a writer. She had let her secret out—again, another risk that she had forced herself to do—and everyone had been supportive. "Yeah, I did. And I sent some query letters out. I'm also thinking about self-publishing, so I might do that as well. You know, it's not like you can choose to be traditionally published but from what I understand, it's a really good deal on the indie publishing too, so I'm excited."

He rubbed his thumbs over the backs of her hands as he held on. "I'm really proud of you. And I think it's great. I've made some changes too."

She couldn't breathe. Hope welled inside her. That was dangerous. "Oh yeah?" It came out wobbly and almost a whisper.

He nodded. "I have. You see, I've been on the

road for a long time. And I grew up longing for that life…longing for adventure and I made my dreams come true. I am one of the most successful stuntmen out there. When I get the hankering to go jump off a mountain or bridge or out of a place, I can do it. But, Gigi, the only thing I long for now is you. I've been longing for you every day, every second since I've been gone. My very smart brother Adam who, growing up, had similar longings in his quest to be a doctor, told me that dreams can change and you can change your life. And, Gigi, that's what I've done. You're looking at the new owner of a piece of property on the outskirts of Sunset Bay that will be the Tate Sinclair Stunt Academy. I'm going to still do some stunts but I'm hoping that when I do that, my wife might be ready to go on a little trip and travel with me a little bit. And if she's not, then I won't. But what I'm telling you, Gigi, is…"

Gigi was having trouble believing what he was saying. She was in shock and when he suddenly went down on one knee, she took a step back. But he held on to her hands. He looked up at her, his face so, so dear.

"Gigi, I am here to stay. If you don't want me to risk and go on stunts, then I won't. I am content. What I want is for you to marry me. I'm asking you to marry me but I'm promising you that you don't have to worry that I'm giving up something that I can't live without because, Gigi, you're what I can't live without. So, will you marry me?"

"Tate, are you sure? Because I can't do that to you."

"Didn't you hear me say that I'm only longing for you now, nothing else? Maybe some babies between you and me—I could long for that. I'm ready to come home. I'm ready to settle down with you. I'm ready to make our dreams come true. I'm ready to watch you fly. I'm ready to see what we can do together. If you'll take a risk on me, I can promise you I'm a really safe bet right now."

Goldie yapped and jumped into Tate's lap, sitting on his knee, and looked up at her. The pup cocked her head to the side as if saying, *Come on, do this.*

But Gigi didn't need the encouragement. Her heart

opened up in that moment, as her world did also. "Yes. Yes, I will marry you, because I've been longing for you, too, and I want to start a life with you. An adventure we'll do together."

He stood up and she stepped into his open arms; they wrapped around her, strong, secure, and with the promise of forever as he lowered his head to hers. Their lips met in a kiss.

A kiss full of toe-curling, heart-pounding love that filled every dark, lonely corner of her world with light and hope and the love she'd been longing for all of her life. Gigi gave herself completely in that moment and knew that from that moment on, she and Tate were one. And she was excited for what the future held.

Because, together, she was ready for anything.

More Books by Debra Clopton

Sunset Bay Romance
Longing for Forever (Book 1)
Longing for a Hero (Book 2)
Longing for Love (Book 3)
Longing for Ever-After (Book 4)
Longing for You (Book 5)

Texas Brides & Bachelors
Heart of a Cowboy (Book 1)
Trust of a Cowboy (Book 2)
True Love of a Cowboy (Book 3)

New Horizon Ranch Series
Her Texas Cowboy (Book 1)
Rafe (Book 2)
Chase (Book 3)
Ty (Book 4)
Dalton (Book 5)
Treb (Book 6)
Maddie's Secret Baby (Book 7)
Austin (Book 8)

Cowboys of Ransom Creek
Her Cowboy Hero (Book 1)
The Cowboy's Bride for Hire (Book 2)
Cooper: Charmed by the Cowboy (Book 3)
Shane: The Cowboy's Junk-Store Princess (Book 4)
Vance: Her Second-Chance Cowboy (Book 5)
Drake: The Cowboy and Maisy Love (Book 6)
Brice: Not Quite Looking for a Family (Book 7)

Turner Creek Ranch Series
Treasure Me, Cowboy (Book 1)
Rescue Me, Cowboy (Book 2)
Complete Me, Cowboy (Book 3)
Sweet Talk Me, Cowboy (Book 4)

Texas Matchmaker Series
Dream With Me, Cowboy (Book 1)
Be My Love, Cowboy (Book 2)
This Heart's Yours, Cowboy (Book 3)
Hold Me, Cowboy (Book 4)
Be Mine, Cowboy (Book 5)
Operation: Married by Christmas (Book 6)
Cherish Me, Cowboy (Book 7)
Surprise Me, Cowboy (Book 8)
Serenade Me, Cowboy (Book 9)
Return To Me, Cowboy (Book 10)
Love Me, Cowboy (Book 11)
Ride With Me, Cowboy (Book 12)
Dance With Me, Cowboy (Book 13)

Windswept Bay Series
From This Moment On (Book 1)
Somewhere With You (Book 2)
With This Kiss (Book 3)
Forever and For Always (Book 4)
Holding Out For Love (Book 5)
With This Ring (Book 6)
With This Promise (Book 7)
With This Pledge (Book 8)
With This Wish (Book 9)
With This Forever (Book 10)
With This Vow (Book 11)

About the Author

Bestselling author Debra Clopton has sold over 2.5 million books. Her book OPERATION: MARRIED BY CHRISTMAS has been optioned for an ABC Family Movie. Debra is known for her contemporary, western romances, Texas cowboys and feisty heroines. Sweet romance and humor are always intertwined to make readers smile. A sixth generation Texan she lives with her husband on a ranch deep in the heart of Texas. She loves being contacted by readers.

Visit Debra's website at www.debraclopton.com

Sign up for Debra's newsletter at
www.debraclopton.com/contest/

Check out her Facebook at
www.facebook.com/debra.clopton.5

Follow her on Twitter at @debraclopton

Contact her at debraclopton@ymail.com

If you enjoyed reading *Longing for You* I would appreciate it if you would help others enjoy this book, too.

Recommend it. Please help other readers find this book by recommending it to friends, reader's groups and discussion boards.

Review it. Please tell other readers why you liked this book by reviewing it on the retail site you purchased it from or Goodreads. If you do write a review, please send an email to debraclopton@ymail.com so I can thank you with a personal email. Or visit me at: www.debraclopton.com.

CPSIA information can be obtained
at www.ICGtesting.com
Printed in the USA
BVHW040049300920
589952BV00022B/532

9 781646 259335